A FIGHTING CHANCE

The five Crow braves stood up and watched Jack Pike approach their camp. As he got closer he saw the one with the scar on his face.

"You have been bothering my woman," Pike said to them in their own language. "You will stop."

"And if we do not?" Scar-Face asked.

"I will kill you."

Pike had his Hawken resting carelessly in the crook of his arm. In his belt was his Kentucky pistol. He could take care of two braves with the guns, but there wouldn't be time to reload. From there he'd have to depend on his knife and his brute strength.

"You cannot kill us all," Scar-Face said, shaking his head.

"Be foolish," Pike said. *"Try me!"*

MOUNTAIN JACK PIKE

JOSEPH MEEK

PINNACLE BOOKS
WINDSOR PUBLISHING CORP.

PINNACLE BOOKS

are published by

Windsor Publishing Corp.
475 Park Avenue South
New York, NY 10016

First printing: September, 1988

Printed in the United States of America

Prologue

I

Naked, Jack Pike stepped out the cabin door. The freezing cold air on his bare flesh made him feel truly alive. It was the reason he loved the mountains. The air in the Rockies was like nowhere else in the country—or, he was willing to bet, in the world.

But even Pike, who thrived on the cold, could only take so much, and so he backed into the cabin and shut the door after him.

On the bed Sylvia Bodeen slept. She too was naked, but her lower body was covered by a sheet while her large breasts were bare. The warmth of the stone fireplace filled the cabin and quickly chased the chill from Pike's bones.

Pike stretched his six-foot-four frame until his muscles cried out in protest. It was morning and time for him to leave if he wanted to get to Green River and this year's mountain man rendezvous on time. He had stopped at Sylvia's for the night only, although she had tried to get him to agree to stay longer.

Sylvia stirred. It was her turn to stretch, still partially asleep, and he watched her naked breasts rise and shift. Suddenly he remembered how warm it had been in bed with her, and he felt a stirring in his loins. He knew if he got back into bed it would be some time before he would leave again. Maybe, he thought, I should go outside in the cold again.

Sylvia moaned and moved her legs at this point, and the sheet fell off, revealing the golden, furry patch between her legs.

"Oh, what the hell," Pike said aloud, and crawled back into bed with her.

"Mmm," she moaned dreamily, as his lips found first one nipple and then the other. "Ooh, Jack . . . what a way to wake up."

"The only way," he said.

Sylvia spread her arms and legs, opening herself up totally to Pike.

Pike concentrated on her breasts for a long time and then started his mouth on a trip downward. When Sylvia had been a young woman, she had always had a flat, taut belly, but the years had added some extra pounds there—which Pike did not find the least bit unattractive. Quite the contrary, since Pike himself was a big man, he preferred his women larger, with more meat on them.

He kissed the extra flesh of her belly, then teased her navel with his tongue. Moving lower still, he rubbed his nose in the rough hair of her pubic bush, then probed with his tongue until he found her wet and ready.

"Oh God, Jack!" she cried out, reaching convulsively for his head.

He circled her core, teasing her, and when he felt her

belly begin to tremble with her approaching orgasm he raised himself and plunged into her.

"Ooh, Jack, you're splitting me apart!"

"Want me to stop?" he asked, whispering the question into her ear.

"No, no, no, no," she babbled, and wrapped her arms and legs around him as if she were afraid that he would really stop.

As far as Jack Pike was concerned, however, there was absolutely no danger of that.

Jack Pike and Sylvia Bodeen were old friends. In fact, Jack and Sylvia's husband, Eddie Bodeen, had been friends long before Eddie married Sylvia. After Eddie was killed in a fight with Zack Lembeck, Pike hunted Lembeck and exacted vengeance for himself and for Sylvia. It was not until almost three years after Eddie had been killed that Pike and Sylvia first slept together. While Eddie had been alive, it had simply never entered either of their minds to do so.

Now, five years after Eddie's death, Sylvia still lived in the old cabin that Eddie had built for them—with Pike's help. It was the only real home she had ever known, and she refused to leave it. Whenever Pike had to pass her cabin on Bear Lake—or pass within a reasonable distance—he always stopped in and spent at least one night. Usually they had dinner, shared some whiskey and talked about the only other person either of them had ever loved—Eddie Bodeen. After that, they'd go to bed.

It took a full six months before Pike stopped feeling guilty the morning after, and Sylvia confided that it had taken her four months.

For people who only saw each other three or four times a year, Pike and Sylvia were the best of friends.

"Do you have to leave now?" Sylvia asked, watching Pike dress.

"I should have left an hour ago."

"No," Sylvia said, "I meant do you really have to leave today?"

"If I want to get to Green River in time I do."

She shook her head and said, "You mountain men and your damned rendezvous. Is this one so important that you can't get there a day late."

Pike stopped dressing and stared at Sylvia Bodeen seriously.

"To tell you the truth, Sylvia, it is rather important."

"Why?"

"Because . . . I have the feeling that we may be approaching the end of the rendezvous. In fact, this might even be the last one."

"You said that last year!"

"The beaver are getting real scarce, Sylvia—"

Annoyed, Sylvia pulled the sheet up to her neck, covering herself, and said, "You said that last year, too."

Now Pike stared at Sylvia with concern.

"What's wrong, Sylvia?"

"Nothing," she said, pouting. "Go to your damned rendezvous."

"No," he said, moving to the bed and sitting next to her. "Seriously, what's the matter? Why are you acting like this?"

She hesitated a moment and then answered.

"There's a Crow camp near here."

"The Crow? This far—"

"There are only five of them, but they . . . come here sometimes."

"What for? To trade?"

"No," she said, biting her lip.

"Then for what?"

She looked him in the eyes and said, "For me."

Pike saddled his horse and thought about what Sylvia had told him.

The Crow had shown up about three months ago, just standing out front one morning when she came out. That first day they did trade with her, but two days later they came back and made clear what they wanted. Their leader—"A big buck with a scar on his face"—pushed his way into the house and raped her.

"It wasn't so bad," she said. "I mean, it's not like I ain't never had a man before." The look on her face, however, belied her words. Even a trollop would be horrified at the prospect of rape. It was much more than simply violation of a woman's body.

After that they came two or three times a week, and one of them would push into the house and take her.

"At least they never all did one after the other," she said.

More often than not, the one who took her was the buck with the scar, but every so often he'd let one of the others have her.

"I thought about killing them, but I wouldn't get one of them before the others got me. I've also thought about killing myself . . . but I knew that eventually you would come."

She told him where the Crow camp was—she'd gone looking for them once, when she was thinking about killing them—and although it was out of his way, he mounted up and headed for it.

He felt he had to do this for her before he went to rendezvous.

A man had to have priorities.

II

He found the camp with no problem and rode straight in, bold as you please. The five Crow braves stood up and watched him approach. As he got closer, he saw the one with the scar on his face.

"What do you want, white man?" Scar-Face asked.

"You have been bothering my woman," Pike said to them in their own language.

Scar-Face smiled and looked at his friends, who were laughing.

"We have been pleasuring her."

"I pleasure her," Pike said. "You have been bothering her. You will stop."

"And if we do not?"

"I will kill you."

"All of us?"

"All of you."

The five braves stopped laughing and studied Pike, as if trying to decide if he would really do it or not.

Pike had his Hawken resting carelessly in the crook of his arm. In his belt was his Kentucky pistol. He would be able to take care of two of the braves, but then the guns would be useless, for he wouldn't have time to reload. From there he'd have to depend on his knife and his brute strength to take care of the remaining three braves.

If it came to that, he felt fairly certain that he'd be able to handle them.

In the end, the final decision would belong to the five Crow.

Pike did what four of the Crow were doing; he watched the fifth man, the leader, Scar-Face. The very first move would belong to him, and when it came, Pike would be ready.

"You cannot kill us all," Scar-Face finally said, shaking his head.

"Be foolish," Pike said. "Try me."

In truth, Pike hoped to be able to bluff the Indians into backing off. However, Pike had never known an Indian to either run a bluff, or run from one. They simply had too much pride for that.

Suddenly, Scar-Face made that move, and the others followed.

As they rushed him, Pike swung the rifle around and fired into the chest of Scar-Face. He immediately discarded that weapon, pulled the pistol and fired again. He knew that he had hit two of them, but there was no time to assess the damage. The other three were almost on him, knives drawn, their lips pulled back tightly against their teeth.

Two of the braves moved to the right of Pike's horse while the third went to the left. Pike launched himself from his saddle to the left, away from the two braves and into the arms of the one.

His weight bore the Indian down to the ground, and he

knew he had only seconds to kill the man before the other two made their way around his horse.

Pike closed his left hand over the brave's right hand, pinning it, and the knife it held, to the ground. He then pulled his own knife and thrust it deeply into the squirming brave's belly. When the knife had penetrated, he pulled it to the left, successfully opening the man's belly to the cold. Something tumbled to the cold ground and lay there, steaming, as the man died.

He was just turning away from the dead Indian when the other two were upon him.

Now it was their weight that bore him to the ground, but even as he was falling back with them, he knew what he was going to do next.

As they landed, he grabbed the Indian whose head was closest to him and bit his ear, clamping down with his teeth as if he were a hungry wolf. The Indian howled and tried to roll away from the pain. Pike held fast for a second until he felt flesh tear, then released the mangled ear. At the same time he felt the second Indian's knife open him up on the left side. Now that his right hand was free, he quickly clubbed the Indian on the side of the head with the handle of his knife before the man could cut him again.

He did not know the extent of his own wound and did not have time to take stock. He lunged to his feet, as the Indian was trying to regain his balance, and quickly slashed his knife across the man's throat. The Crow screamed, but the sound was muffled by the blood that was welling up in his throat. He dropped his knife and used both hands to try and staunch the flow of blood from his mouth and from the neck wound.

Pike turned quickly to face the Indian whose ear he had

almost bitten off. The move caused pain to lance through his wounded side.

The Indian, bleeding profusely from the ear—which appeared to be hanging by a thread—stood up straight and faced Pike. Pike, the taste of the man's blood still sharp and brackish in his mouth, waited for the Crow to make the first move.

The Crow had other plans, however. He obviously realized that Pike's wound was the more serious one, and was producing more blood loss. If he could wait Pike out, then the white man might grow weak from loss of blood.

Pike could almost read the man's mind and knew now that he would have to make the first move.

"Your friends are dead," he said to the man in his own language. "Go now, and live."

"I will kill you like the dog that you are," the Indian replied. "And then I will cut off your ears and wear them around my neck."

"You will die," Pike said. "Of this there is no doubt."

Pike was the taller of the two, but the brave was strongly built. He was, in fact, probably the strongest of the original five braves. Pike could not be certain that his own strength would be superior.

However, he would soon find out.

Apparently, Pike's words and the mocking tone of his voice had agitated the brave; for when Pike moved, so did the Indian, and they came together like two grapplers.

Pike's left hand closed over the Indian's right wrist as the Indian's right hand closed over Pike's right wrist. They stood this way for a few long moments, strength against strength, each man trying to bring his knife hand into play.

As Pike had suspected, the Indian's strength was at

least equal to his. Neither man was able to gain an advantage, and the sticky blood that was covering him reminded Pike that he desperately needed that advantage—and soon.

Both men had their legs braced, each taking the pressure in their powerful thighs. Suddenly, Pike released the pressure of his right leg, causing the brave to fall into him. As he did so, Pike lifted that knee and slammed it hard into the brave's belly. The air exploded from the man's lungs with a great "whoosh," and Pike felt the man's hold on his wrist loosen sufficiently.

He finally had his advantage.

He pulled his right hand free, which threw the brave even farther off balance, and then lunged with the knife, planting it firmly in the man's sternum. The brave's face registered shock and disbelief, and then all life just faded from his eyes. Pike stepped back, pulled his knife free and let the man fall to the ground.

Before checking on his own wound, Pike quickly surveyed the damage he had wrought. Both of his initial shots had travelled truly, striking their targets in the general vicinity of the heart—certainly close enough for the fifty-caliber balls to cause death.

He checked the third and fourth braves and found them good and dead also. Satisfied that all five were dead, he finally lifted his buckskin jacket and calico shirt to check the damage. As it turned out, the wound was fairly superficial, the extent of the bleedings no indication as to the wound's seriousness, which was minor. He would clean and treat the wound as best he could when he reached a stream.

He had successfully defended Sylvia's honor, and soon

enough she would realize that she needn't expect any further visits from the five Crow.

Now it was time for rendezvous.

Part One

RENDEZVOUS

One

"When is Pike supposed to get here?" "Whiskey" Sam Benedict asked.

"You've got me," Rocky Victor said.

"He is coming, isn't he?" "Skins" McConnell asked.

"Have you ever known Pike to miss a rendezvous?" "Trapper" Jim Cooper asked.

"Not since he started worrying that every one might be the last one," Whiskey Sam replied.

"Worry wart," McConnell said, scoffing. "As long as there are mountain men, there'll be rendezvous."

"And as long as we're around, there'll be mountain men, huh?" Jim Cooper asked.

Benedict and Victor were old timers in the true sense of the word. Both of them could have been in their fifties or sixties, except neither of them was saying. Each had grey in his hair and beard, Whiskey Sam more than Rocky. They also both had leathery skin from years of exposure to the cold and the sun, but then most of the mountain men had that. They both wore old skins, and it was a toss up as to which of them had bathed last—if they had at all that month.

Jim Cooper and Skins McConnell were of the same age

group as Jack Pike. In fact, McConnell was the closest thing Pike had to a friend these days.

"How do you think Pike is going to react when he finds out that Fitz is booshway?" Cooper asked.

"I hope he whups him," Benedict said.

"Do you think he could?" Rocky Victor asked.

Benedict laughed. "It would be a good fight, you can bet on that."

"My money would be on Pike," McConnell said. "Fitzsimmons is a strutting peacock."

"Speak of the devil," Whiskey Sam said, and they all turned to watch Fitz walk by, proudly wearing his badge of office.

"Somebody should strangle him with it," Whiskey Sam said.

"Somebody might," Skins McConnell replied.

Dan Fitzsimmons adjusted the "gorget," his symbol of office, around his neck. The crescent-shaped metal neckpiece stamped him as booshway of this particular rendezvous, a position of power he had long been waiting to attain. He intended to make the most of it—for himself.

Fitzsimmons left his tent and walked through the confusion which was rendezvous.

Around him men stood in groups, some dressed casually, others taking this opportunity to dress in all their finery, especially the older trappers. Even the Indians dressed in the gaudiest cloth they could afford.

He passed the group of Benedict, Victor, Cooper and McConnell and ignored them. He knew they didn't like him, but that only made them even. He also knew that they were waiting for the arrival of their hero, Jack Pike.

He was waiting for Pike to arrive, too. If there were ever two men on the planet who hated each other, they were Pike and Fitzsimmons, and Fitzsimmons couldn't wait for Pike to see the gorget around his neck.

Fitzsimmons continued through camp, examining all the women who were present. The one he finally settled on was a pilgrim, here for the first time to assist her husband, who was a merchant who had come from St. Louis for the gathering. She was tall and dark, with silky black hair and smooth skin.

She would be the one, he decided.

His first official act.

Caroline Hennessy saw the big mountain man watching her. He was tall and broad, dressed in clean buckskins and wearing an odd-shaped piece of metal around his neck. He stared at her, and she held his gaze boldly.

"Caroline! "

Her husband's voice called from within the tent which was his temporary general store.

"Coming, Arthur," she said. She held the bearded man's stare a moment longer, then went inside.

"Arthur, what does it mean when a man is wearing a crescent-shaped piece of metal around his neck?"

Arthur Hennessy looked up from his inventory. He was a tall, slender man with thinning sandy hair and a habit of squinting at people over his spectacles. He'd often wondered what a beautiful woman like Caroline had seen in him to make her marry him.

"That's a gorget," he said. "IT's worn by the booshway as a symbol of his authority."

"The booshway? "

"He's the man who officiates at the rendezvous."

"What is a gorget?"

"It's a French term, actually. It was the last vestige of a nobleman's armor and has evolved into the symbol of the mountain man's authority at rendezvous."

"So the man wearing it is the boss?"

"So to speak. He will officiate at whatever contests are to be held."

"Is he the, uh, local police chief?"

"Not really. The dog soldiers are the real police."

"Who are they?"

"The Indians you see walking around with arm bands. Dear, I don't really have time to answer all these questions. Perhaps later—"

"Of course," she said. "What did you call me in here for?"

"I need your help with this inventory."

"Sure," she said, looking bored. "That's what I'm here for, isn't it?"

Briefly, she thought about the man who had been watching her.

The booshway.

The man in charge.

She liked men who took charge.

Fitzsimmons was waiting outside when Caroline Hennessy came out again a half hour later.

"Hello," he said.

She turned, startled, and then relaxed when she saw him.

"Oh, hello."

"Is this your first rendezvous?"

"Why yes, it is."

"My name is Fitzsimmons," he said. "Dan Fitzsimmons. I'm the booshway."

"I know."

"You know? How do you know?"

She caught his gaze and held it boldly. "I asked."

"Oh, you did, did you?"

"Yes, I did."

"Would you like me to show you around camp?"

"I would like that very much, Mr. Fitzsimmons."

"That is, if your husband doesn't mind."

"Mind? Why should he mind?" she asked. "He's in there busy with his inventory."

"Well, then," he said, "allow me to give you the tour."

Pike paused atop the ridge and looked down at the rendezvous camp. This was always one of the most exciting times of the year for him, and he could never quite put his finger on exactly why. Ever since his first rendezvous back in '25, he'd looked forward to this all year.

He and Eddie Bodeen had attended that first rendezvous together.

The first time he'd ever met Sylvia Bodeen was at a rendezvous, back in '29.

It was at a rendezvous that Pike had caught up with Zack Lembeck, back in '32.

Good memories and bad memories. That was the thing about rendezvous.

You never knew what was going to happen.

Two

Pike rode into camp and immediately saw the foursome of Whiskey Sam, Rocky Victor, Jim Cooper and Skins McConnell. He waved and rode over to them.

"What took you so long, Pike?" Benedict asked. "You're usually the first one here."

"Hello, Sam," Pike said, leaning over in his saddle to shake the leathery old hand.

"Pike," Rocky Victor said. Pike shook hands with Victor and Cooper. He merely nodded to Skins McConnell because Skins was the closest thing he'd had to a friend since Eddie Bodeen.

"Pike," Skins said. "Good to see you."

"You're looking good, Skins."

"Get that horse taken care of, and we'll get us a drink," Whiskey Sam said. It was not for nothing that he was called "Whiskey."

"I'll do that," Pike said. "Be back in a few minutes."

At the far end of camp, a place had been set up for the care of horses. In fact, the horses were picketed far enough away from camp so that nothing that happened in camp would spook them.

Pike removed his gear from his saddle, including the

skins he had brought along for trade, and then turned his horse over to one of the men who'd been designated for the job. Walking away, he did not give the animal a second thought. He didn't even care if he didn't get the same animal back at the end of rendezvous. He'd known a lot of men who had named their horses, but he never saw the sense in naming an animal he might one day have to eat to stay alive.

He was walking back to meet the others when he heard the sounds of a struggle. He stopped and listened.

"I said no! " he heard a woman say sharply.

"Sure, now you say no," a man's voice said. "Earlier, all you had on your mind was yes—ow!"

As the man cried out in pain, Pike put a name to the voice. It was Dan Fitzsimmons, and from the sound of it, he had a woman with him who didn't want to be with him.

He dropped his gear to the ground and followed the sounds of the voices.

By the time Caroline Hennessy realized that she made a mistake by going with Fitzsimmons, it was too late—or at least, she thought it was. When she saw the huge man come around the side of the tent, she gasped at the size of him. Fitzsimmons saw the man too and released her. She backed away and looked at the men, the two biggest men she had ever seen in one place at one time.

And they were going to fight.

Over her.

She moved to a safe distance and settled down to watch, her breath coming quickly.

* * *

"What do you want, Pike?" Fitzsimmons demanded.

"Thought I heard a woman in distress, Fitzy," Pike replied.

"Nobody here needs your help."

"Is that true, ma'am?" Pike asked, looking at the woman. Even over the tension of the moment he noticed what a beauty she was.

"No," she said. "I wanted to leave, and Mr. Fitzsimmons was insisting I stay."

"Hear that?" Pike said to Fitz. He was about to say something else when he noticed something that took him by surprise.

"Shit," he said, staring at Fitzsimmons' neck.

"What's the matter, Pike?" Fitzsimmons asked. "Never seen a gorget before?"

"I never thought I'd see it around your neck," Pike said. "It's almost blasphemous."

"Just keep walking, Pike. This ain't none of your affair."

"Just because you happen to be booshway, Fitzy, that don't mean you can have any woman in camp if she don't want to be had."

"Shit," Fitzsimmons said. "If it don't mean that, what does it mean?"

"That's the shame of it," Pike said, shaking his head. "You really don't know, do you?"

Pike walked away from Fitzsimmons toward the woman and said, "Come along, Miss—"

"Look out!" Caroline cried out, as Fitzsimmons made a move to strike Pike from behind.

Pike turned quickly and warded off the blow. In one swift move, he hooked his fingers in the chain of the gorget and tore it from Fitzsimmons' neck.

"I expected a move like that from a weasel like you," he said, holding the gorget in his hand. "You don't deserve to wear this."

Fitzsimmons laughed. "It'll take more than your word to make me give it up."

Pike grinned tightly and tossed the gorget to the woman, who deftly caught it.

"I hadn't intended to use words."

Three

For the second time in a matter of days Pike found himself facing a dangerous man in hand-to-hand combat.

In the case of Fitzsimmons, this moment had been coming for a long time. The two men had never liked each other, and that dislike had gradually grown into pure, unadulterated hatred.

Now it was going to explode.

"Come on, Pike," Fitzsimmons said. "We might as well get this over with right at the beginning."

Pike was suddenly aware of how bone tired he was, not only from all the riding, but from the battle with the five Crow braves. If he was going to win this fight—if he was going to avoid being seriously hurt by Fitzsimmons—he was going to have to incapacitate the man quickly.

Fitzsimmons came toward him, and Pike contented himself to stand and wait for him. Dan Fitzsimmons was a big man, but Pike figured he had the edge in height and weight just a little. He wasn't all that sure about speed. He'd seen Fitzsimmons fight younger, seemingly faster men, and end up hurting them. In fact, he once saw the undeserving booshway cripple a man with his bare hands.

Now Fitzsimmons advanced on him, not recklessly, but very deliberately. The look in his eyes was one of pure meanness.

Pike wondered if that was where Fitzsimmons ultimately had the edge. He wondered if he could ever be as vicious a man as Fitzsimmons was—even to Fitzsimmons, himself.

The time for thinking and wondering was over.

Fitzsimmons closed on Pike, and the two men grappled for a moment, looking for an edge. When none was forthcoming, they broke apart and began to circle one another. For a moment, Pike thought back to the last of the five Crow braves and wondered how Fitzsimmons would have fared against the brave.

At this point, a man walking by noticed what was happening and excitedly ran to shout it to the rest of the camp.

Watching a good fight was one of the favorite pastimes at rendezvous.

A crowd gathered in seconds, and at the forefront were Jim Cooper, Rocky Victor, Skins McConnell and Whiskey Sam Benedict. There were also some dog soldiers watching, but as far as they were concerned, it was not their job to stop a fight in which the booshway himself was involved.

"Well, here's your chance," Whiskey Sam said to Skins McConnell.

"What chance?"

"You said your money would be on Pike."

"You want to be on Fitzsimmons?" Jim Cooper asked in disbelief.

"I want to bet," Whiskey Sam said, "and I know none of *you* are going to bet on Fitz."

"All right," McConnell said. "I've got a dollar that says Pike wins."

"I'll go for a dollar," Rocky Victor said to Whiskey Sam.

"Can you cover all of this?" Jim Cooper asked. "You want in for a dollar?"

"Yep."

"No problem," Whiskey Sam said. "Besides, it would be worth three dollars to me to see Dan Fitzsimmons finally get a whupping."

All bets down, they settled back to watch the fight.

Pike was getting tired. He had to admit it. After all, he'd been dead tired when he'd ridden in and had been looking forward to a meal and some sleep, not a fight—and certainly not a fight of this magnitude.

They'd been trading punches for about fifteen minutes, and even though Fitzsimmons had a cut over his left eye and a bloody nose, he didn't show any signs of fatigue.

Pike's arms felt like he was wearing lead gloves; his mouth was cut, and he had a cut beneath his right eye. The only advantage he had left was that the blood from Fitzsimmons's cut was flowing into his eye, and the man had to constantly try to clear it. Every time he did, Pike would snap another punch out, usually connecting.

He had always felt that beneath his beard Fitzsimmons had a cast iron jaw. He was now certain of it. His right hand ached from hitting it.

So he changed targets.

As Fitzsimmons lashed out with a punch, Pike tensed to take it, at the same time launching a right hand of his own. As Fitzsimmons' punch landed flush on Pike's jaw, rattling his teeth, his own punch landed squarely in Fitzsimmons's belly.

"Ooh," Skins McConnell yelled, grabbing his belly. "*I* felt that one myself."

"It's about time Pike decided to hit something other than Fitzsimmons' face," Jim Cooper said.

"Pike is weakening," Benedict said. "His punches don't have that same snap."

"You gotta remember," McConnell said, "he just rode in. He hasn't even had a chance to rest, yet."

"He should have thought of that before he started this," Whiskey Sam said.

"Who says he started it?" McConnell asked.

"From what I here," Whiskey Sam said, "they's fighting over that woman over there."

Four sets of eyes shifted to the woman in question.

"Jesus," Rocky Victor said, "she's worth fighting over, ain't she?"

"That she is," McConnell said, staring at the woman with obvious appreciation.

"She's also married to that St. Louis feller," Whiskey Sam said.

"Which St. Louis fella?" Cooper asked.

"Hennessy."

"How does he expect to hang on to a woman like that?" McConnell asked.

"Maybe he don't," Whiskey Sam said. "Maybe this here fight is winner take all."

"Well, we may find out soon enough," Cooper said. "I don't know how much longer these two can keep it up."

"Pike will keep it up as long as he has to," McConnell said. "You wait and see."

While I, McConnell said to himself, wait and hope.

Four

Caroline Hennessy watched the two men exchange blows. The man who had come to her rescue—to rescue her from her own folly, as it turned out—didn't know her, and yet he was taking part in this brutal battle for her benefit.

Or so she thought.

Knowing nothing of the history of the two men, she couldn't know that this fight might as well have been occurring over a knife, or a chicken leg. These two men were bound to come to this, but for the moment Caroline Hennessy found herself sexually excited by the entire incident.

In the crowd she saw her husband watching the fight and knew she'd have to think of something to tell him. She also knew, however, that whether the man who had come to her aid won or lost, he'd need some nursing, and she intended to be that nurse.

She wanted noting more than to touch him, to put her hands on his body. She'd never wanted to touch a man so badly before in her life.

If only she could convince Arthur to go about his business when it was all over, so she could be alone with the man.

After five minutes of being pounded in the stomach, Fitzsimmons began to back up for the first time.

Pike felt a swelling over his right eye and was afraid that one more good punch would bust him wide open. Fortunately, Fitzsimmons chose that time to start going for Pike's body, digging punches into his stomach and ribs.

"Now see," McConnell said to Whiskey Sam, "Pike could pound on Fitz's head all day and get nowhere, but going to his body is driving him back. Fitz would have been better off to keep hitting Pike in the head—see that swelling over Pike's eye?—but now he's hitting Pike in the body. Jesus, he could hit Pike there all day and do no damage. You ever see Pike with his shirt off?"

"Him and me ain't that close," Whiskey Sam said.

"You can't hurt that man hitting him in the body," McConnell said. "Wait and see."

Fitzsimmons dug a punch to Pike's body, and Pike felt the knife cut put there by the Crow brave split open and start bleeding again.

Great.

"Pike's bleeding from the side," Whiskey Sam said. "See it?"

"Yeah," McConnell said.

"Bleeding like a stuck pig," Jim Cooper added with concern. "That ain't from no punch."

"That's from something we don't know nothing about," McConnell said. "That's serious."

"Maybe we should stop this thing," Rocky Victor said.

"Go ahead," Whiskey Sam said. "Stop it and I win three dollars."

"We try and stop it, and they'll turn on us," McConnell said. "We'll just have to wait and see what happens."

The punches to his body weren't hurting him, but Pike knew that pretty soon he'd grow weak from loss of blood—not that he wasn't already weak. It was only pure stubbornness that was keeping him going, just like it was pure meanness that was keeping Fitzsimmons going.

Pike hit Fitzsimmons in the belly again, and he felt the man shudder. The body blows were getting to him.

At that point Fitzsimmons decided to turn the fight into a wrestling match. He lowered his head and tackled Pike around the waist, bringing them both to the ground.

"Ooh, Pike's down!" Whiskey Sam exclaimed.

"Yeah, and who's that on top of him?" McConnell asked. "They're both down."

"Who's the better wrestler?" Jim Cooper asked.

Nobody answered.

Pike knew that Fitzsimmons was trying to get his arms around him in a bear hug, and he didn't relish the thought. He drew his head back and then butted Fitzsimmons on the bridge of the nose.

"Jeez!" Fitzsimmons shouted, rolling away from Pike.

Pike didn't know if he'd broken the man's nose or not, and he didn't wait to find out. He stood up, and while Fitzsimmons was hunched over, he punched the man behind the left ear. Fitzsimmons shuddered and staggered but didn't go down. Pike followed him and punched him in the kidney, which drove Fitzsimmons down to one knee. After that, Pike hit him once, twice, and then a third time behind the ear, and Fitzsimmons finally went down, sprawling on his face in the dirt.

"That's it!" McConnell whooped. He turned to Cooper and said, "Collect for me," and hurried to Pike to keep his friend from falling down next to Fitzsimmons.

Caroline Hennessy caught her breath when Pike walked

over to her and took the gorget from her hands. The brush of his fingers made her entire body tingle.

Pike walked to where Fitzsimmons lay and dropped the gorget onto his broad back. He might have fallen himself if Skins McConnell hadn't come to his side and taken hold of his arm.

"Thanks," McConnell said.

"For what?" Pike asked, breathlessly.

"I just won a dollar on you."

"Jesus," Pike said, "I went through this for a dollar?"

"Three," McConnell said. "Rocky and Jim also won."

"Well," Pike said, "that's different."

Five

"Are you all right?" Caroline Hennessy asked Pike.

Both Pike and McConnell turned and looked at her, and even in his bruised and battered state, Pike recognized an aroused woman when he saw one—a *beautiful,* aroused woman.

"I'll be fine."

"You have to let me help you."

"Caroline!"

She closed her eyes at the sound of her husband's voice and pretended not the hear.

"Caroline," Arthur Hennessy said, coming up next to her. "Come, dear, it's all over."

"I have to help this man, Arthur."

"I'll be fine," Pike said.

"Why must you help him?" Hennessy asked.

"Really," Pike said, "I'm fine."

"He was fighting for me."

"For you?"

"That man was accosting me," she said, pointing to the fallen Fitzsimmons. There were several men crouched over him, but he hadn't moved yet. "This man saved me."

"Well, in that case," Arthur Hennessy said, "we are in

your debt, sir. Perhaps you will allow us to see to the treatment of your wounds."

"Really," Pike said, "that's not necessary—"

"We can take him back to the tent," Caroline said.

"I have a tent," Pike said, and then looked to McConnell for confirmation. They had agreed that whichever was first to arrive would get a tent for both of them. McConnell nodded to indicate that he had been able to do this.

"All right," she said. "Go to your tent. I'll get some water and cloth and be right there."

"No, really—" Pike began, but both husband and wife had turned and hurried away.

"Better watch out for that woman, Pike."

"Yeah. . . ."

"What the hell happened to your side?"

"I'll tell you later," Pike said. "Let's get to the damn tent so I can sit down."

When they reached the tent, McConnell set Pike down on one of two cots. He noticed that McConnell had somehow appropriated a small potbelly wood burner for them. Jim Cooper entered after them, carrying Pike's gear.

"Here's your dollar," he said to McConnell.

"Didn't anybody place a bet for me?" Pike complained.

"In all the excitement, we didn't think of it," McConnell said, pocketing the money.

"Who bet against me?"

"Whiskey Sam," Cooper said.

"That figures," Pike said. "That old—" He was interrupted by the appearance of the woman, who had not yet been introduced to him. She was carrying a pan of water and several cloths.

"I'll thank you gentlemen to leave now," she said to McConnell and Cooper. "I have to clean his wounds."

McConnell and Cooper exchanged glances, and then McConnell said, "When you can get to your feet, we'll buy you a drink."

"It's the least that you can do."

They left, and Caroline knelt down next to him.

"Let's get this off," she said, reaching for his shirt.

"We haven't been introduced yet," he complained.

"My name is Caroline Hennessy."

"I'm Jack Pike."

"Now, let's get this off," she said. She helped him off with his buckskins and shirt, and he saw her take a moment to examine his torso.

"How did this happen?" she asked, touching his side. The bleeding had slowed, but the wound was still seeping.

"A disagreement with an Indian's knife."

"You fought that man even though you knew you had this wound?"

"I didn't have much of a choice."

She touched him then, her fingers long and graceful, cool against his skin. First she ran her hand over his side, across his abdomen, the hard slab of his chest, and then his face. He saw her breathing quicken, and he himself was reacting to the closeness of her in the small tent.

"You going to use that water before it gets cold?" he asked her.

She pulled her hand away from him first as if she'd been burned, then laughed. She picked up one of the cloths and went to dip it in the water.

"It's probably already cold."

She used the wet cloth and cleaned the blood from his face and his side.

"Would you like me to make some kind of bandage for the cut under your eye."

"No," he said. "It'll be all right. Let the air hit it. Nothing cures like Rocky Mountain air."

"You like the Rockies?"

"I love them. What about you?"

She shrugged and wet the cloth again. "It's cold."

"It is at night, but during the day with the sun out, it's actually quite nice."

Quite nice, to Pike, meant somewhere in the high thirties.

She finished cleaning him up and then fell back onto her heels, examining him.

"How do I look?"

She laughed. "I'd love to see you on a St. Louis street."

"Not me," he said, shaking his head and reaching for his shirt. "Not in a city."

"Have you ever been to a city?"

"I have, and cities and I don't get along."

As he started to put his shirt on, she said, "Would you like me to wash that for you?"

"No," he said. "Wash your husband's shirts, Mrs. Hennessy."

She looked at him and said, "Caroline," and held his gaze.

Pike knew he had to get this woman out of his tent before something happened. He stood up, and she put the used cloths together and stood up with the basin of water.

"I appreciate this," he said.

"It was the least I could do, after what you did for me," she replied.

"How did you get into that situation, anyway?"

She shrugged and said, "Bad judgement."

She touched his arm then, and he said, "The same kind of judgement you're showing right now?"

"No," she said, closing her hand over his right forearm, "this is not bad judgement, Pike." It seemed right to her to call him Pike instead of Jack.

"Mrs. Hennessy—"

"Caroline."

"Caroline . . . no, this isn't right. Your husband—"

"Forget my husband."

"I can't."

"You will," she said, and kissed him.

For one dizzying moment, as her full lips pressed against his, he did forget her husband, but abruptly the man—whom he didn't think he'd recognize if he saw him again—came lurching back into the tent—not physically, but spiritually—and came between them.

He put his hand against her belly and pushed her away from him.

"You will forget him," she said again, and left the tent.

Part Two

MURDER

Six

Pike found Skins McConnell, Jim Cooper, Rocky Victor and Whiskey Sam in the tent that had been set up as a saloon. A couple of wooden doors had been set up on barrels as a bar, and the foursome was standing there enjoying beer.

"Is it cold?"

"Not yet," Skins said, "but they promise it will be by tomorrow."

Pike slapped Whiskey Sam on the back hard enough to make the man choke on his beer.

"Sorry I cost you three dollars, Sam."

Whiskey Sam started sputtering and spraying beer and said, "Christ, ya damn near cost me my life now, choking me that way!"

"I'll buy you another one."

"Ya damn right ya will. Barkeep!"

The bartender came and took their order, and by the time he brought them each a beer, Whiskey Sam's disposition had changed.

"I tell ya," he said, "it was worth three dollars to see Fitz get a whuppin' like that."

"Yeah, well, he's not the only one who got a whipping," Pike said, touching the cut beneath his eye gingerly.

"Ah, he never laid a hand on you," Whiskey Sam said.

"Pike, was I you, I'd keep an eye on Fitz the rest of the time we're here," Jim Cooper said.

"Fitz ain't gonna shoot him in the back, if that's what you're thinkin'," Whiskey Sam said.

"I wouldn't put it past him," Cooper said.

"No, I think Sam's right," Pike said. "If anything, Fitz would want another try at me."

"Why?" McConnell asked. "You beat him fair and square, and you weren't even at your best. Next time it won't take you half as long."

"Don't underestimate Fitzsimmons," Pike said. "He may be mean, vicious and—"

"Dumb?" McConnell asked.

"No, he's not dumb, he's just . . ."

"You can't even think of a word, can you?" McConnell asked.

"He's low, but he's not a killer—not from behind, anyway," Pike said. "Besides, he's booshway this year."

"What's that mean?" McConnell asked. "He'll try to rape a woman, but not kill a man?"

"I don't think he was raping her."

"You know something we don't know?" McConnell asked, looking interested.

"No," Pike said, looking away from his friend's probing eyes. "I just think there was a misunderstanding between them, that's all."

"You mean like he wanted to rape her, and she didn't want to be raped?" Cooper asked, and the others laughed.

"Don't know why he'd want to rape a woman, anyway,"

commented Whiskey Sam. "They's plenty of squaws around who'd like with you willin' like."

"Did you see that woman?" Rocky Victor asked. "Or are your eyes goin'?"

"I seen her. So?"

"So?" Victor said. "You can look at a woman what looks like that and say so? You're getting older than I thought you was, Sam."

"I'm the same age you are, you old coot," Whiskey Sam said. "And don't you forget it. Besides, which of us brought his own squaw with him."

"Was that a squaw you brung?" Rocky Victor asked. "I thought that was your pack mule!"

From behind, McConnell said, "Let's take a walk while they argue."

When they left, Cooper was trying to get between Whiskey Sam and Rocky Victor.

Outside it was dark, and the air had taken on a distinct bite. Pike, however, still wore just his buckskins. McConnell had on a light jacket with a fur collar.

"Do you want to fill me in?" McConnell asked.

"On what?"

"Well, for starters, that wound on your side. You didn't get that saving some lady's virtue, did you?"

"Well," Pike said, rubbing the side of his jaw, "as a matter of fact, I did."

Pike told McConnell about Sylvia and the five Crow braves.

"You killed all five?" McConnell asked. "That's impressive, even for you."

"I got lucky," Pike said. "Besides, I didn't exactly come out of it without a scratch, did I?"

"If that scratch is all you got for facing five Indians

alone, then you did get lucky," McConnell said. "My God, man, do you want to die?"

"What are you so het up about?"

"Because I value you as a friend, Pike, and I don't like to see my friends trying to commit suicide," McConnell said tightly. "First fighting five Crow braves, and then Dan Fitzsimmons, fresh from the trail with no rest and a wound to boot. It seems to me, my friend, that you're using up more than your quota of luck."

Pike stared at McConnell for a few moments and then said, "I think you're right."

McConnell was taken aback. "You do?"

"Yes."

"No argument?"

"None. It was a fool thing fighting Fitzsimmons like that, over a strange woman."

"Ha," McConnell said. "There isn't anything strange about that woman; she's only the finest looking lady I've seen in a long time."

"That's not saying much," Pike said, "considering all we see up here are worn-out squaws, but I agree. She is very beautiful."

"And married."

"I know that."

"I mean, not that her husband would be any threat to you physically, but who knows? Maybe *he's* the type to try and shoot you in the back."

"Well, he won't have any reason to."

"You're going to stay away from his wife?"

"I am."

"And is she going to stay away from you?"

Pike hesitated a moment and then said, "I sure hope so."

"Tell me something, Pike."

"What?"

"What was she doing with Fitz?"

"She says she showed bad judgment."

"That's putting it mildly," McConnell said. "Well, all I can say is, don't you do the same thing."

"Tell me something," Pike said in a conspiratorial whisper.

"What?"

"Where did you get that wood burner that's in our tent?"

Seven

"I don't think you should, Arthur," Caroline Hennessy said.

"But you're my wife, and the man was accosting you," Arthur Hennessy said.

"But he's already been punished."

"Not by me," Hennessy said, straightening his back. "You're my wife, not *that* man's." Hennessy paused to slip into his coat. "I'll go and find that man Fitzsimmons and thrash him."

"Arthur, you can't—"

"I was the boxing champ at my school," he said. "I can take care of myself."

"Arthur—"

"I'll be back soon," he said.

Their tent was large and divided into two sections. The front was the store, and the back—the smaller portion—was where they slept. He went through the flap that separated the back from the front, then walked through the store section and out into the night.

Caroline put a shawl around her shoulders and followed. She had to find Pike before Arthur got hurt.

* * *

"Your face looks like shit," said the man from the fur company.

"Never mind my face," Fitzsimmons said. "What about these skins?"

"They're high grade, all right," the man said, "but I can get high grade from the others, as well."

"Not in the quantity I can get for you."

"What did you do," the man asked, "find a beaver mine?"

"And not at my prices."

"No, that much is true," the man said. "What would your friends and colleagues think if they found out you were undercutting them?"

"I have neither," Fitzsimmons said. "Do we have a deal?"

"If you can deliver the quantity you say," the man said, "then we have a deal."

Fitzsimmons nodded in satisfaction and said, "Don't you worry. I can deliver."

Hennessy went to Fitzsimmons' tent, and when he didn't find him there, he settled down to wait for him. He had not boxed for many years, and in his mind he now went through his moves.

The two men he had seen in battle today had shown no sign of any formal training. Arthur Hennessy—though smaller by far than both those men—felt sure he'd have no trouble teaching Fitzsimmons a lesson.

* * *

"Pike?"

Pike looked at McConnell and asked, "What does that sound like to you?"

"Trouble," McConnell said without hesitation.

Both men stood up in their tent as the voice called out again, more urgently, "Pike!"

"Yeah!"

Pike stepped outside, followed by McConnell, and both saw Caroline Hennessy.

"Caroline," Pike said, "what are you—"

"It's Arthur," she said, cutting him off, "my husband."

"What about him?"

"He's gone after Fitzsimmons."

Pike looked at McConnell.

"I've seen Hennessy," McConnell said. "No offense, ma'am, but Fitz will kill him."

"That's what I'm afraid of," she said. "Can you do something?" she asked Pike.

"Let's go," Pike said to McConnell.

Fitzsimmons' mind was elsewhere when he approached his tent and was accosted by Arthur Hennessy.

"Mr. Fitzsimmons."

"Wha—" Fitzsimmons began, but before he could focus on Hennessy, the smaller man punched him in the face. The punch startled more than jarred Fitzsimmons, but it did open a cut on his lip that had been put there by Pike.

"What the hell?" he said, touching his bleeding lip.

"I would advise you to stay away from my wife from now on, or face more of the same," Arthur Hennessy warned.

"Your wife?"

"Yes, the woman you tried to rape this afternoon. I am her husband."

"You little—" Fitzsimmons said, and punched Hennessy in the face.

Hennessy almost flew through the air, landing on his butt in the dirt, his head spinning. Before he could collect himself, Fitzsimmons hauled him to his feet and hit him in the stomach. Hennessy promptly threw up on Fitzsimmons, which only made the larger man angrier. He held Hennessy by the shirtfront and began to methodically hit him in the face and body.

Suddenly, Fitzsimmons was grabbed from behind and pulled off balance. He released his hold on Hennessy, and the man fell to the ground. As Fitzsimmons regained his balance, he saw Pike and McConnell, and the Hennessy woman crouched down next to her husband.

"What the hell do you want?" Fitzsimmons asked Pike. "You want some more?"

"I don't think you could take any more, Fitzsy," Pike said. He looked at McConnell and added, "Not from the both of us."

"That little man had it coming. He hit me for no reason at all."

"Oh, I think he had a reason, Fitz," McConnell said.

"Arthur," Caroline Hennessy said, raising her husband's head off the ground. She saw cuts above and below both eyes, and a mouth that was almost mashed. In addition, his nose might have been broken. There was no telling yet what injuries he might have sustained to the body.

"Help me get him up," she said to Pike and McConnell.

"You'd better be on your way, Fitz," Pike said. "We'll take care of Hennessy."

"Just keep him out of my way!" Fitz warned, and walked away toward his tent.

"Let's get him up," Pike said.

"Jesus," McConnell said, reaching for the man's arm as Caroline moved out of the way, "he's a mess."

"He sure is," Pike said.

Eight

They took Hennessy back to his tent, and Caroline directed them into the back.

"I'll have to clean him up," she said, making it sound like a chore.

"Well, you've got experience with that, don't you?" Pike asked.

"Yes, I do."

"I think we'd better get back—" McConnell started to say, but Caroline cut him off.

"Pike, would you stay awhile?" she asked. "I'd like to talk to you."

McConnell said, "I think we'd better—"

"It's very important."

"Go ahead, Skins," Pike said. "I'll be along."

As McConnell left, Caroline said, "It'll just take me a few moments to clean him up and get him to bed."

"All right."

While she took care of her husband, Pike looked around. He was impressed by Hennessy's stock, and even more impressed that they had come all this way carrying it to sell it to the mountain men who would gather here for rendezvous. For the first time in a while, Pike once again wondered if this would be the very last rendezvous. He hoped not.

Caroline reappeared, lowering the sleeves of her shirt. He noticed that the top three buttons of the shirt were undone, and he could see the tops of her breasts.

"What was it you wanted to talk to me about?" he asked.

"Would you like some coffee?"

"I don't think so."

"I could make some."

"No, thanks."

"All right," she said, "I'll come to the point. I think my husband and I might need a bodyguard while we're here."

"What makes you say that?"

She looked surprised. "You saw what Fitzsimmons did to my husband. And what about what he did to me this afternoon?"

"Almost did."

"Well, he would have done it if you hadn't come along."

"I'm not so sure."

"What? What are you suggesting?"

"I'm suggesting," Pike said, "that Fitz might have had some provocation for what he did."

"Are you saying I led him on?"

"That's what I'm saying."

She regarded him for a few moments, then smiled slowly and said, "Well, maybe you're right. I might have led him on a bit, but I certainly have a right to change my mind, don't I?"

"You're a woman, aren't you?"

"Yes, I am," she said, moving closer to him. "How nice of you to notice."

"Do you love your husband, Mrs. Hennessy?"

"I thought you were going to call me Caroline."

"For this question, I think Mrs. Hennessy is more appropriate. Don't you?"

"Yes," she said, "yes, I do love my husband."

"Then why would you—"

"I have a roving eye, Pike," she said. "I admit it. Arthur is not a very large man, and all of you mountain men are so . . . big—especially you."

"There are bigger men than me."

"I haven't seen any," she said. "I'm fascinated by you, Pike."

"That's very flattering."

"Aren't you . . . attracted to me?"

"That's a fool question," he said. "Of course I'm attracted to you, but you're married."

"Does that matter up here?"

"Why should up here be any different from down where you come from."

"Well, you don't see many women around here, do you?" she asked. "I would have thought that an opportunity to be with a woman would—"

"There are plenty of women up here, Caroline," Pike said. "In fact, you'll see some of them here in camp."

"You mean . . . the Indian squaws?"

"That's right. Some of the men have even brought their squaws with them, like Whiskey Sam. Other squaws come here to find men."

"But what about a white woman?"

"A white woman would be . . . nice," he admitted, looking her up and down. "Especially one who looks like you."

"I see," she said, moving closer still. Her breasts bumped into his chest, and she stayed there, pressing them against him. As if they had a mind of their own, his hands moved around her, first touching her back and then moving down to cup her buttocks. He could feel the heat of her groin right through both of their clothing . . . and then suddenly, as her mouth was inches from his, he remembered her husband.

"No," he said, stepping back.

She laughed, a sound that came from deep within her, a rich, lovely sound that sent chills up and down his spine.

"You see?" she said.

He cleared his throat and asked, "See what?"

"I told you that you'd forget him," she said. "You almost did this time. Next time, you will."

She laughed again, and he took the sound of it outside with him and back to his tent.

When Pike reached his tent, he decided to walk around in the cold a little more. When that didn't help his condition, he entered his tent. Skins McConnell looked up curiously.

"Well?"

"Well what?"

"Was it important?" McConnell asked, propping himself up on his elbows.

Pike shrugged. "She just wanted to make a point," he said, starting to undress to turn in.

"And did she?"

Pike turned away so that McConnell wouldn't see the raging erection he still had that even the cold mountain air couldn't do anything to wilt.

"Yeah," Pike said, "she made it, all right."

* * *

Caroline Hennessy watched her sleeping husband for a few moments. Getting into bed with him now would be useless—but then even healthy Arthur Hennessy was basically useless in bed. He was a very nice man, a decent sort; he loved her and he treated her well, but she'd always had to find physical gratification elsewhere.

She reached for her shawl, put it around her shoulders and left the tent.

The man entered Dan Fitzsimmons tent quietly. He waited a moment while his eyes adjusted to the moonless dark, then drew his knife and advanced on the figure wrapped in a blanket.

The man stood above Fitzsimmons for a few moments, letting his hatred fuel his resolve, and then leaned over and drove his knife through the blanket into the man's back. The sleeping man didn't make a sound. The attacker withdrew his knife, then leaned over and pulled the blanket away from his victim's face. Even in the dark he could see that it was Fitzsimmons, and that he was dead.

Satisfied, the man cleaned his knife on the blanket and then left.

Nine

Pike woke the next morning to the sounds of shouting and running feet pounding past his tent. He looked around and saw that McConnell was also coming awake.

"What the hell is going on?" McConnell asked. "It sounds like a stampede."

Pike shrugged and standing, started to dress.

"Let's find out," he suggested, and McConnell nodded and also started to dress.

Fully dressed they stepped out of their tent, squinting against the bright glare of the morning sun. Even the sunlight seemed purer to Pike atop the Rockies.

A dog soldier came running by, and Pike reached out and closed a large hand over the man's arm, stopping him in his tracks.

"What's going on?"

The man looked at Pike with wide eyes, as if he didn't comprehend.

"Come on, man," Pike said, shaking the man. "What's happened?"

"The booshway," the Indian said.

"What about him?"

"He is dead."

Pike looked at McConnell really quick and said, "Fitz-simmons?"

"Please, I must go," the dog soldier said.

"Where?"

The man hesitated a moment, then said quite frankly, "I do not know."

Pike opened his hand and said, "Go," and the Indian started running again.

"They're all running around like chickens without heads," McConnell observed.

"They don't know what to do."

"Do we?"

"Yes," Pike said. "Let's go to Fitzsimmons' tent and find out how he died."

"I hope it was a heart attack," McConnell said.

"Why's that?"

"Because if he was killed," McConnell said, "guess who everybody is gonna think done it."

Pike didn't have to guess.

He knew.

When they reached the tent, there were some dog soldiers milling about outside. They also saw Jim Cooper talking to a man who looked familiar.

"Is that—" McConnell started to say.

"Yes, it is," Pike said. "That's Jim Bridger."

Bridger was a legend among mountain men as a trapper and as a trail blazer. It was only natural that the people in camp would hover about him in a time of crisis.

Pike and McConnell approached Bridger and Cooper,

both of whom sported the first name Jim. To avoid confusion, Pike had already decided to address each man by his last name.

"Pike," Cooper said, seeing him approaching.

At the sound of the name, Bridger turned and smiled. "Hello, Pike," he said.

Jim Bridger was about Pike's age and was at least as tall while being rangy rather than brawny. Still, there was a lot of strength in his firm handshake.

"Bridger," Pike said. Both men shook hands. They were not good friends, but there was a mutual respect between them that, in a way, was even better.

"What's going on?" McConnell asked.

"Jim Bridger, this is Skins McConnell," Pike said.

"Pleasure," Bridger said, shaking hands with McConnell. "I've heard some nice things about you."

"You have?" McConnell asked in surprise, but Bridger had already turned his attention to Pike again.

"Seems like our booshway has got himself murdered," Bridger said.

"Murdered, how?"

"Stabbed twice in the back."

"Jesus," Pike said. "In his sleep?"

"Looks that way." In annoyance Bridger looked at the people who were milling around them or simply running about. "Can't we do something about these people?"

"We can get some dog soldiers to keep them away from the tent," Pike said. "That'll give them something to do, as well."

"Well, let's do it, then," Bridger said. "Can you take care of that, Coop?"

"Sure, Jim," Cooper said.

Bridger looked at Pike. "I'm glad you're here, Pike," he said. "We need some cooler heads."

"When did you get in?" Pike asked Bridger.

"About a half hour ago. I asked somebody who the booshway was and then came here looking for him."

"You found him, then?"

Bridger nodded.

"Let me take a look," Pike said.

Bridger and Pike both entered the tent as McConnell moved away to try and help Cooper restore order to the camp.

"That's the way I found him," Bridger said.

Fitzsimmons was lying on his stomach, and Pike could see the blood that had soaked through the blanket. He leaned over to examine the body and satisfy himself that the man was indeed dead. He lifted the blanket and looked underneath, then let it settle back down on the body.

"We'll have to handle this ourselves, Pike." Bridger said. "We can send somebody for some law, but it would take a while."

"You propose to try and find the killer yourself?" Pike asked.

"No," Bridger said, "I propose the *we* try and find the killer *our*selves."

"You and me?"

"All of us, but I guess the rest of the people up here would look to us for some guidance, Pike. Don't you?"

Pike knew that was true. He knew how the others looked at him and Bridger, as larger than life men who would take charge of any given situation.

"There'll have to be a new booshway," Pike said.

"Who's next in line?"

"I don't know," Pike said. "Let's ask Cooper."

Both men stepped out of the tent and saw that some semblance of order had been restored. There were a few dog soldiers herding people away from the tent, and McConnell and Cooper were approaching.

"Coop, we we're just wondering who would be next in line as booshway. We're going to need someone to stand in authority," Pike said.

In spite of the seriousness of the situation, Cooper had to smile.

"What's so funny?" Pike asked.

"The man who's next in line as booshway."

"Well, who is it?"

Cooper looked at all three men to be sure that he had their attention, and then said, "Whiskey Sam."

The Indian squaw was not pretty, and she was some years past her prime; but she had large breasts with big nipples, and she knew how to bring a man to readiness, even when he was more than a little past his prime.

The woman was crouched between the legs of Whiskey Sam, rolling his penis between her breasts, which shone with sweat, and alternately licking it and sucking it. Slowly but surely Whiskey Sam was coming erect. Shit, the old man remembered days when he used to wake up hard as a rock and ride a squaw for hours before finishing. These days it was a constant struggle to get it hard, and then he usually shot his load just seconds after entry. Still, it was the only way to start a day. Hell, when the time came he couldn't mount his squaw first thing in the morning, he'd be the first one to put a bullet in his head.

"Sam!" a voice shouted from outside.

"Jesus," Whiskey Sam said. His teeth were clenched as he watched the squaw work on him.

"Sam, I'm coming in," he heard the voice of Jack Pike call.

He was acutely aware of his naked potbelly and his spindly legs covered with wiry, white hair. The squaw was covered pretty much, with only her big breasts bare. She looked up at him as if for guidance as to whether to stop or continue.

"Sam," Pike said, sticking his head into the tent.

"Tarnation!" Whiskey Sam snapped. "Can't a man even wake up in the morning before people start poking their heads into his tent?"

Pike looked at the woman's breasts with disinterest, and then looked at Whiskey Sam's face.

"Trouble, Sam. You'd better wake up later."

"What kind of trouble?"

"Fitzsimmons is dead."

"So? Hell, you trying to tell me he didn't deserve to die?"

"Not stabbed in the back while he was asleep."

"What?"

Sam sat up and pushed the squaw away. She covered her breasts and stared at Pike with huge, cowlike eyes. Now, if only she had a man like that to wake up in the morning.

"The booshway's dead, Sam, and we need a new one."

"What's that got to do with me?"

Pike tossed him something and said, "You're next in line. Get dressed and come on out here. You're in charge now."

Sam looked down at what Pike tossed him and found

that he had caught the gorget, which he had last seen around Dan Fitzsimmons' neck.

"Jesus Christ," he said.

Ten

Whiskey Sam dropped the blanket back down on Fitz-simmons and stood up.

"Well, he's dead, all right," he said, looking at Pike and Bridger. "Let's step outside."

Pike was impressed with Whiskey Sam's reaction to suddenly having authority pushed onto him. When he came out of his tent wearing the gorget, he looked like a totally different man. Despite his name, Sam had never really been a drunk, but he was certainly a cantankerous old cuss who few would have been able to see as booshway at the rendezvous. Even Pike had felt doubt when Cooper had told him that Sam was next in line, but now Pike felt that Sam just might be able to pull it off.

With a little help from his friends, of course.

Outside, Sam looked at Pike, Bridger, Cooper and McConnell.

"We'll have to move the body," he said.

"To where?"

"Bury it, I guess."

"What about when the law shows up?"

"And when's that gonna be?" Sam asked. "We'll bury it shallow, so's it can be dug up again. The cold ground ought to keep it from rottin' too fast. Meanwhile, we got to try and find out who done it."

"Quietly," Pike said.

Sam looked at him. "You got somethin' to say, Pike, go ahead and say it out loud."

"Somebody killed Fitz; there's nothing we can do about that," Pike said. "But I think we've got to keep this rendezvous going. We've got a new booshway, and things should progress normally."

Sam looked at the others and said, "What say you?"

"I agree," Bridger said, and Cooper and McConnell nodded.

"Another thing," Pike said.

"What?" Sam asked.

"There's no reason the whole camp as to know Fitzsimmons was murdered."

"What's the point of keepin' that a secret?" Sam asked.

Pike shrugged. "I don't rightly know. Maybe it'll keep the killer nervous."

"You think the killer is still here?"

"Well, if he let camp after killing Fitzsimmons, that'd be like a confession," Pike said. "Yeah, I think he's still here."

"Sounds right to me," Bridger said.

"All right," Sam said. "Let's wrap Fitz in a clean blanket and make sure nobody sees the other one. We'll have some dog soldiers dig a shallow grave and drop him into it. Coop, why don't you go along and make sure they don't peek at the body? They'll spread the news sure as shit if they find out."

"All right," Cooper said.

"I suppose findin' the killer is gonna be up to us, huh?" Sam said, looking at the four men. He rubbed his hand over his grey-white stubble and then said, "Pike , I'd like to talk to you in private."

"Sure, Sam."

"I'm going to get settled in," Bridger said. "I'll see you later."

"I'll help Coop," McConnell said.

They all went their separate ways, leaving Sam and Pike in front of the tent.

"I ain't cut out for this, Pike," Sam said abruptly.

"You're doing fine, Sam."

"Maybe, but how's everyone else gonna feel when they find out I'm booshway?"

"If Bridger, and Skins, and Coop and I accept it, they will, too."

"What about Rocky?" Sam asked.

"He's your best friend, Sam."

"That old—" Sam started, then stopped. 'Yeah, I guess you're right. He's the only other one we'll tell about this, all right?"

"We'll all help you, Sam. You can count on us."

"I know," Sam said. "I know I can." He peered up at Pike and said, "Think it's too early for a drink?"

"Coffee," Pike said.

Sam looked at Pike dubiously, then said, "Coffee, huh?"

Pike nodded. "Coffee."

When Arthur Hennessy awoke that morning, his head felt as if it weighed a ton.

"Jesus," he said, putting his hands to his head.

"Arthur?"

He looked up at Caroline.

"I brought you some tea," she said, kneeling next to him with the cup in hand.

"Thank you."

"How do you feel?"

He sipped the tea, hissing as the heat of it touched his swollen lips. "Awful."

"I would have put ice on your face, but you were unconscious most of the night."

"I was asleep," he said with dignity. "Asleep."

"Of course," she said, "you were asleep."

He worked at drinking some of the tea, then looked at her watching him.

"I could have handled him, you know," he said, "but he was quite . . ."

"I know," she said. "He didn't play by the rules."

"If he had fought fairly . . ."

She put her hand on his arm and said, "It was a foolish thing to do, Arthur, but thank you." She leaned over and kissed his cheek, which made him moan. "There is something you should know," she added.

"What?"

"There's been quite a bit of commotion in camp."

"About what?"

"Fitzsimmons is dead."

"What?" he exclaimed and then cried out in pain as a crack at the corner of his mouth opened and began to bleed. "How?" he asked, putting his fingers to the wound.

"I don't know," she replied. "Nobody seems to know, except Pike and some of the others."

"It couldn't have been from what I did," Arthur Hennessy said. "I didn't mean to kill the man."

"I'm sure you didn't," Caroline said. "It's more likely that he died from some wound he received fighting Pike."

"I suppose so," Hennessy said.

"Do you think you can eat some breakfast?"

"I don't know," he said. "Would like to clean up, though."

"Can you stand?"

He handed her back the tea and said, "We'll soon find out, won't we?'

Part Three

THE SHOOT

Eleven

There was to be a shooting contest that day. Originally, as booshway, Dan Fitzsimmons was supposed to officiate at the competition. Now Whiskey Sam would do so.

Over coffee, Whiskey Sam told Pike, "I know most of it is fairly simple—I mean, under normal circumstances."

Bridger, McConnell and Jim Cooper were also having coffee. McConnell and Cooper had come in late, having seen to the burial of Dan Fitzsimmons.

"It's this murder, though," Sam said. "I'm not sure how to handle this. I mean, I ain't no lawman, you know."

"None of us are, Sam," Pike said.

"Anybody got any idea how to proceed?" McConnell asked.

"I could try to handle that part for you, Sam," Pike offered. "I mean, we all could."

Bridger cleared his throat and caught everyone's attention.

"I don't think that's such a good idea, Pike," Bridger said. "I mean, for you to be looking into Fitzsimmons' death."

"Why is that?" Pike asked.

"Well, I haven't been here all that long, but already I've heard about the fight you and he had yesterday."

"So?"

Bridger smiled and said, "Sounds like it was a real humdinger. I'm sorry I missed it."

"Sorry I can't say the same," Pike said. "I'm sorry I didn't miss it. Get to the point."

"Now, don't take offense, Pike, but if it does get out that Fitzsimmons didn't die of natural causes, who do you think everyone is going to think killed him?"

Pike looked at McConnell, who had already suggested the very same thing.

"In fact," Bridger said, "under those circumstances, it might not even be wise to keep from everyone else the fact that he was murdered."

McConnell spoke up before Pike could. "They might think we were covering for you, Pike," he said. "I mean, look at the people at this table. It's no secret that we're all your friends."

Pike did as McConnell said. He looked at all the men at the table with him. It might have occurred to him to become angry at the suggestion—if he hadn't seen the sense to it, that is.

"What do you suggest, then?"

"Even though he's buried already," Bridger said, "I think we ought to call some people in—you know, a representative of all the groups we've got here, mountain men, merchants, dog soldiers, whoever's here from the big companies—and tell them what's happened. Now somebody's first reaction is going to be to accuse you. I mean, there's a big mouth in every bunch, right?"

"You're telling it," Pike said.

McConnell was keeping a wary eye on Pike, to see how he was going to take all of this.

"I think that's when Sam here ought to get up and explain as how the killing is going to be looked into and the guilty party brought to justice—no matter who he is."

"So, you don't think Sam ought to come right out and say he doesn't think I did it."

"No," Bridger said.

Pike looked at Sam, "You think I did it, Sam?"

"To tell you the truth, Pike," Sam said, "I would think you done it if he hadn't been stabbed in the back. That ain't the way you'd kill a man."

"Well, thanks for that anyway," Pike said. He looked around the table and asked, "Anybody feel different?"

"Nobody here thinks you done it, Pike," McConnell said.

"But we can't say that; is that what you're saying, Bridger?"

"Pike," Bridger said, "if we don't come right out and defend you, it might make the real killer feel safe, you know? Maybe he'll make a mistake."

Pike thought it over and nodded. "Okay," he said, "okay then, I'll go along—but I want you all to know that I'm going to be nosing around, unofficial like."

"That's fine, Pike," Sam said. "If it was any other way, I'd be asking you to be the one to do the nosin'."

"Who you gonna ask now?" McConnell asked. "Bridger?"

Sam looked at Bridger.

Bridger looked at Pike.

"We know each other, Pike," Bridger said, "even respect each other, but do people see us as being friends? I mean, the way you and Skins here are?"

"No," Pike said. He looked at Whiskey Sam and said, "I think Bridger's the one, Sam. There aren't too many people who would complain about him."

"Except for that big mouth in every bunch," McConnell said.

"Yeah," Pike said, lifting his coffee high, "here's to the big mouth, whoever he is."

They all toasted the as yet unknown big mouth, and then Sam said, "Anybody got any ideas?"

"About what?" Cooper asked.

"About who did kill Fitzsimmons," Sam said. "I mean, who would kill him that way?"

"Somebody who was afraid to try it face to face," Pike said. "Who's he been having trouble with since he arrived?"

"Who hasn't he been," McConnell asked. "As soon as enough people got here, he started pushing his weight around, looking at all the women like he was picking out his favorite."

"Like the Hennessy woman?" Pike asked.

"Yeah, like the Hennessy woman," McConnell said.

"Tell me about her," Bridger said. "And about the fight."

Pike looked at McConnell, who took the hint and told the story.

"When you see the woman," he finished, "you'll understand."

"What about the husband?"

McConnell told Bridger about the husband bracing Fitzsimmons and taking a beating for it.

"What *about* him, then?" Bridger asked. "Could he have killed Fitzsimmons, either to avenge his wife, or himself?"

"He might have, except for one thing," Pike said.

"What's that?"

"I don't thing the sonofabitch could have walked that far from his own tent."

Twelve

After they finished their coffee, they dispersed, each going his own way. McConnell, Pike and Bridger were all to compete in the shooting contest later in the day. They had decided that they'd wait until evening and then call a meeting to talk to some of the people about Fitzsimmons' death.

Outside the saloon tent, where they'd had their coffee, Bridger caught up to McConnell and Pike.

"Can I talk to you, Pike?"

"Sure," Pike said. To McConnell he said, "I'll catch up to you."

After McConnell left, Bridger said, "Look, Pike, if my being here is going to be a problem, I'll butt out right now."

"What makes you think there's going to be a problem? We're all just trying to help Sam."

"I know we're not close friends, Pike," Bridger said, "but I wouldn't want to ruin the friendship that we do have."

"Just do what you said you'd do," Pike said. "I didn't kill Fitzsimmons, Bridger, so we're not going to have a problem. Okay?"

"Okay. Uh, will you be talking to Hennessy today?"

"Probably. Why?"

"Oh, I thought I'd talk to him, but I'll wait until later on."

"I'll just drop in on him and see how he's doing," Pike said. "Any questions about Fitzsimmons can come from you."

"Fair enough."

The two men stood there awkwardly for a moment before Pike broke the silence.

"Look, there's no sense in us feeling awkward about this, Bridger. We both want the same thing, to help Sam and find out who killed Fitzsimmons."

"Agreed."

"All right, then," Pike said, and turned away walking toward his tent . . . feeling awkward.

When Pike reached the tent, McConnell was inside cleaning his rifle, a Hudson's Bay fuke with a thirty-six inch barrel. McConnell considered himself an excellent marksman, but so far he had never been able to beat Pike. In fact, the only man who had ever beat Pike was Bridger, but that happened only once. Pike had outshot men like Kit Carson and Jim Beckworth with regularity. It didn't look to McConnell like either of those men would be here this year—at least, not in time for the shooting contest.

"You ready for the shoot?" McConnell asked.

"I'll be there," Pike said, "but I want to talk to Hennessy first." He picked up his Hawken, his pouch and his powder horn and started out again.

"Pike?"

"Yeah."

"I hope I didn't, uh, say anything that, you know, insulted you or anything."

"No, you didn't."

"I was just trying to, uh, you know—"

"I know," Pike said. "Help Sam."

"Right."

"We're all trying to do that, Skins."

"I don't think you did it."

"Thanks."

"I could, uh, say that you were in the tent with me all night."

"That's true, I was, but we were both asleep, weren't we?"

"Well, yes—"

"And I couldn't swear that you were in the tent all night, so how could you swear I was?"

"I could just . . . you know, swear," McConnell said, concentrating on the barrel of his rifle.

"Skins, look at me!"

McConnell looked up.

"There's no need to lie for me. I didn't kill Fitzsimmons."

"I know that."

"Then if Bridger or anyone else asks, just tell them the truth. Okay?"

"Okay. Don't get sore."

"I'm not sore!"

"I'm gonna beat you this year, you know," McConnell called out as Pike was leaving the tent.

"Yeah, sure."

Pike went over to the Hennessy's tent where he found Caroline working behind the counter. Arthur Hennessy was nowhere in sight. He was either out, or he was in the back lying down. Pike's money said he was flat on his back after the beating he took from Fitzsimmons.

"Good morning," Pike said.

Caroline looked up and smiled when she saw him. The smile transformed not only her face, but the inside of the tent. It was like a new sun had come out. Suddenly, Pike felt nervous.

" 'Morning. Did you sleep well?"

"I slept all right," he said. "How about you?"

She shrugged.

"How is your husband?"

"He's still lying down. He tried to get up this morning, but he couldn't. I think he might have some broken ribs."

"I could look at him, if you like."

She seemed to take that into consideration for a moment, then nodded and said, "Okay. Come on."

She led him into the back.

"Arthur, Mr. Pike is here. He's offered to check your ribs."

"Is he a doctor?" Hennessy asked.

"No," Pike replied, "just somebody who's trying to help. If you don't want it—"

"Why not?" Hennessy said from his cot. "You've been very helpful so far, hasn't he, Caroline?"

"Yes, he has, Arthur."

Pike stared at Hennessy for a few moments and then decided that maybe the man was just a little embarrassed. His ego was bruised because Pike had saved his wife from Fitzsimmons while giving the man a beating, and then Hennessy, who felt that *he* had to stand up for his wife, *took* a beating from Fitzsimmons. He had to feel awkward being in the same room with Pike and Caroline.

"Open your shirt," Pike said, crouching down next to Hennessy.

Hennessy obeyed, and Pike probed his ribs while the man hissed in pain.

"I don't think they're broken," Pike finally said, standing up. "Just heavily bruised."

"What if they are broken?" Caroline asked.

"Not much you can do for broken ribs but let them heal by themselves."

"That means staying off his feet, right?"

"For a while, yes."

"I can't do that," Hennessy said. "I have business to do."

"I can take care of the business, Arthur."

"You don't know—" Hennessy said, starting to rise but he gasped and fell onto his back as a wave of pain hit him.

"I know how to sell, and take money," Caroline said. "That's what you're worried about, isn't it, Arthur. Losing money?"

"If losing money was all I was worried about, I wouldn't be laying here, would I?"

That sounded like pretty good logic to Pike, but Caroline turned on her heel and left.

"Um, you take care," Pike said to Hennessy, and followed Caroline out.

Caroline was behind the counter again, apparently setting up for the day's business.

"Guess he really can't walk, huh?" Pike asked.

"Or do much of anything else, either," Caroline said without looking at him.

If he really couldn't walk, then it couldn't have been him who killed Fitzsimmons.

"Well," Pike said, "I've got a shooting match to compete in."

She looked at him then and said, "I wish I could come and watch, but I'll be stuck here."

Pike didn't know what to say to that, so he started to leave.

"Pike?"

"Yeah?" He turned and saw her leaning on the counter with her elbows, her face framed and supported by both hands.

"Will you let me know who wins?"

"I won't have to," he said.

"Why not?"

"Because I'll win," he said, and left.

Outside, he felt foolish about the boast and wondered why he had done it.

No, he didn't.

Thirteen

The first stage of the shooting contest was simple. Clay targets were set up at varying distances, and the shooters stood and fired six at a time. There were forty contestants. They were allowed six shots each, and then more if needed, until by the end of the first stage they were cut down to twenty, including Bridger, McConnell, Cooper and Pike.

Whiskey Sam was the official who ruled on the contest, declaring hits and misses, near hits and miss hits. Occasionally the breeze from a passing ball would cause a clay target to jump, creating the illusion of a hit.

"All right," Whiskey Sam shouted, "we have our twenty shooters who will advance to the next round. Everybody take a break and be back here in an hour."

The twenty shooters who were eliminated left the area, looking for a drink or a card game. The others mingled, discussing shots from this round and discussing the next round.

"You're shooting real well this year, Skins," Pike said to his friend.

"I told you I was gonna beat you, didn't I?"

"Bridger's shooting real well, too."

"Yeah, I noticed."

"There's also someone else who's doing real well."

"Yeah, I noticed. Who is he?"

"I don't know," Pike said. "Why don't we find out?"

They walked over to the man in question, who was a newcomer to the rendezvous. He was young and smooth faced, and looked as if he hadn't even started to shave. He was concentrating on his rifle and looked up as they reached him. The rifle was a Leman Indian rifle with a short barrel, about thirty-three inches. The barrel on Pike's Hawken was forty-one inches.

"How do?" the stranger said.

"My name's Jack Pike," Pike said. "This here's Skins McConnell."

"Jack Pike," the younger man said, looking impressed. "I heard of you. I'm Hal Swenson, from Pennsylvania."

"Welcome to rendezvous," Pike said. "What do you think?"

"I think it's great. Everything I heard it would be."

"Heard from who?" Pike asked.

"Louis Washburn."

"L.J. Washburn?" Pike said, looking surprised. "How is old L.J.?"

"He died last year. He was guiding some settlers from Pennsylvania, and they were hit by Indians."

"Were you there?"

Swenson shook his head. "I had come out months before. I met L.J., and he sort of took me under his wing."

"Well, now I don't have to ask you where you learned how to shoot," Pike said.

"Yeah," Swenson said, laughing. "L.J. taught me. He even gave me this rifle."

"I was wondering how you got hold of an Indian rifle."

"L.J. never threw anything away if he thought he could get some use out of it."

"Listen," Pike said, "we've got some time before the next round. Can we buy you a drink?"

"Trying to get me drunk so I can't see straight?"

They all laughed.

"Just one beer each, for fortification."

"Sure, why not?"

They all walked to the saloon tent, where others had already started drinking. Some shooters who had been eliminated were drinking whiskey and razzing the shooters who were still in the running.

"Let's find a barrel," Pike said after they got their beers from the bar. He meant the mostly empty barrels that had been set up as tables, and they found one in the back.

They talked a little bit about L.J. Washburn, who McConnell had not known, so he was regaled with stories about the old man from both Pike and Swenson.

"L.J. was one of the original mountain men," Pike said. "He came out here in the twenties with Jed Smith, carrying a sixty caliber *jaeger* which he modified to fifty caliber to conserve powder."

"He told me about that," Swenson said, and then told a Jedediah Smith/L.J. Washburn anecdote that proved to Pike that he really did know Washburn.

After a moment Swenson looked at Pike and said, "You been testing me, haven't you? I mean, all these stories about old L.J.?"

"Maybe just a little," Pike admitted.

"You satisfied?"

"Yeah, I'm satisfied. No hard feelings, I hope."

"No, no hard feelings," Swenson said. "I'm just glad

to meet somebody who liked the old codger as much as I did."

"You should talk to Whiskey Sam and Rocky Victor while you're here, then," Pike said. "They both knew L.J."

"Will you introduce me?"

"I will, but right now we've got to get back to the line."

They finished their beers and walked back to the line together.

"Fella doing the officiating is Whiskey Sam. He's also booshway."

"I understood Dan Fitzsimmons was booshway," Swenson said. He obviously had not heard about Fitzsimmons' death.

"Fitz had an accident," Pike said.

"What kind—"

"We'd better talk about this later," McConnell interrupted. "Sam's calling shooters to the line."

"Okay," Pike said. He turned to Swenson and said, "Good luck."

"To both of you, too."

As the younger man walked away, McConnell shook his head and said, "They're getting younger all the time."

"That they are, partner."

The second round was speed shooting, and for this they shot only two at a time, because more targets had to be used per person.

Generally, the older marksmen usually prevailed during this round because they knew what they had to do in order to load and fire faster, and get off more shots during the allotted three-minute time period.

When the final ten were announced, Pike was not surprised to see the young Swenson there with himself, McConnell, Cooper, Bridger and some of the other older men. Swenson had obviously learned from L.J. Washburn the trick of keeping extra balls in his mouth, so they'd be readily accessible during loading.

"All right," Whiskey Sam shouted, "second round is over. Third round starts in one hour."

At the end of the second round, Pike and McConnell just hunkered down where they were and set to cleaning their rifles. Swenson came over and asked if he could join them.

"Sure, hunker down," Pike said.

Swenson did so and made a face. "Damn balls taste terrible. I could use another beer."

"Have one," McConnell invited.

"Ha," Swenson laughed. "I will . . . after the contest is over."

They all cleaned their rifles, Pike finishing first, followed by McConnell and then Swenson.

"What's the next round like?" Swenson asked.

Pike and McConnell exchanged glances.

"You're going to like this round," Pike said. "It's real . . . interesting."

"Oh really?" Swenson said. "What's it like?"

"They're setting up for it now," Pike said, inclining his head toward the targets.

Swenson turned and saw that men were imbedding axes in thin slats of wood, so that the blade was facing the shooting line. Then they were hanging a clay target on either side of the axe blade.

"What the—"

"You have to hit both targets with one ball," McConnell said.

"*Both* targets?" Swenson asked. "With *one* ball? How are you supposed to do that?"

"Simple. All you got to do," Pike said, "is make sure your ball hits the axe blade right, is cut in half, and strikes both clay targets."

Swenson gaped, looked at the targets, and then back at Pike.

"Piece of cake," Pike said.

Fourteen

"All right," Whiskey Sam shouted to the crowd that had gathered to watch, "we have ten shooters left. They'll fire two at a time. When there's a miss, the shooter drops out, until there is only one man left."

Swenson was standing next to Pike. He leaned over and asked, "What's the prize? What are we shooting for?"

"Nothing," Pike said. "Whenever we get together here at rendezvous, we don't need an excuse to have a contest. I guess you could say it's just for bragging rights until next year."

"Who won last year?" Swenson asked.

McConnell leaned over and said, "Pike did. In fact, Pike's won the last three years running."

"Who won before that?"

Pike nodded his head and said, "Bridger."

"One year," McConnell added, "and Pike won it the two years before that."

Swenson looked at Pike. "I guess I've got my work cut out for me."

"I think we all do."

"Shooters to the mark!" Sam shouted.

Two men stepped to their marks and fired at their leisure. Both missed, shook their heads and moved away. Neither had hit even one target.

The next four shooters stepped to the mark and walked away with the same result.

That left Pike, McConnell, Bridger and Swenson.

Pike and McConnell stepped to the mark together and fired. Both of their balls struck the axe blade just right. Each ball was cleaved in two, and both clay targets shattered. They moved away to the sound of thunderous applause and whistling.

Bridger and Swenson stepped to the mark and fired, and both men were successful.

"We've got four shooters left," Whiskey Sam announced. "We'll move the targets back ten feet and go again."

Three times all four men fired successfully, and three times the targets were moved back.

"That's over a hundred yards," somebody said aloud.

"I can hit a running buffler at a hundred yards," another man said, "but an axe blade?"

Pike and McConnell stepped up. Pike fired first, cleaving his ball and striking both targets, shattering them.

McConnell fired next. His ball struck the axe blade wrong. Most of it went to the right and struck the clay target; the rest of it went left, and everyone saw the target jump but remain intact.

"Shit!" McConnell said as Whiskey Sam walked to the target. Everyone waited while he inspected it, and then he turned and waved his arms in a negative fashion.

A piece of the ball had struck near enough to the clay target to make it move, but had not actually struck it.

"No hit!" Sam shouted, returning to his previous position. "Pike is in; McConnell is out."

McConnell turned to Pike and said, "I guess I'll have to wait until next year to beat you."

"I guess so," Pike said. "Good shooting, Skins."

"Yeah," McConnell said, and went to join the spectators. Several man patted him on the back and congratulated him for some fine shooting.

Now Bridger and Swenson stepped up to their marks. Swenson fired first, and both clay targets shattered. As everyone applauded, Bridger waited for the din to die down, lined up his shot and fired.

And missed.

He missed the target completely, and everyone just stared.

"Son of a gun," he said. He shook Swenson's hand and then moved away through the crowd.

He didn't stay to watch the final two men shoot. He knew that most of the people in camp would be watching, though. He even saw Caroline Hennessy, who had been pointed out to him earlier.

He walked through the crowd and made his way to the Hennessy tent.

He wanted to talk to Arthur Hennessy without interruption.

He could always try to win the shoot again next year.

"What are you accusing me of?" Arthur Hennessy asked Bridger.

"I'm not accusing you of anything, Mr. Hennessy," Bridger said. "I'm just asking if you went to see Fitzsimmons again during the night?"

"How could I?" the man demanded from his cot. "I couldn't move. Still can't, thanks to him."

"I'm sorry you were injured—"

"You a friend of Pike's?"

"Uh, we know each other."

"You know, the more I think about it, the more certain I am that he stood and watched Fitzsimmons pound me. He could have stopped it earlier, but he waited until I was badly hurt to step in."

"Now why would Pike do that?"

"Ha!" Hennessy said. "I've seen the way he looks at my wife."

"You'll excuse me for saying this, Mr. Hennessy," Bridger said, "but I've seen your wife; and I'm sure there are many men in camp who look at her when she walks by."

"Yes, well, none of *them* played the big hero to her the way Pike did. You know how women react to that sort of thing."

"As I heard it, you also acted heroically."

"Sure," Hennessy said, "but I was the one who was beaten up. It was Pike who whipped Fitzsimmons."

"So you did not see Fitzsimmons after your, uh, altercation?"

"How many times do I have to tell you no?" Hennessy demanded, sitting up in bed. He glared at Bridger, then seemed to remember that he was in pain and laid back down.

"All right, Mr. Hennessy," Bridger said, "thanks for your time."

"Hey," Hennessy said as Bridger was leaving.

"Yes?"

"Why are you asking all these questions. I thought Fitzsimmons just . . . died."

"Oh, he's real dead, all right," Bridger said, and left before Hennessy could ask any more questions.

Dead maybe, Hennessy thought, but he didn't *just* die. Not if the famed Jim Bridger is asking questions.

Fifteen

"It's too damn far away now to even see," someone in the crowd complained.

Pike and Swenson had each fired four more times, successfully. The crowd was getting edgy, and Whiskey Sam was going hoarse.

"Would you fellers please settle this thing here and now?" he asked before they fired a fifth time. That brought some laughter from the onlookers.

Pike and Swenson exchanged glances. Pike was impressed with the young man's ability, and his calm. So much so that he wondered if Swenson hadn't actually known about the axe target all along. Maybe he'd heard about it from Jed Smith.

Pike stepped to the line, and Swenson watched him along with the rest of them. He fired. His ball wavered, struck the blade wrong, and its entire mass veered right and shattered that clay target.

"A miss!" Whiskey Sam shouted excitedly. It had come to the point where he didn't care who won, just so it was over with, at last.

The people in the crowd had a different view. Most of them had bet on Pike and, although they were waiting for it to be over, wanted it to be finished with him declared the winner.

Now, as Swenson stepped to the mark, the people with money on Pike watched nervously. Pike watched the youngster with more admiration as he cooly lined up his shot, fired . . . and missed.

His ball struck the axe blade all right, but when it ricocheted off, it missed clay completely.

"A clear miss!" Whiskey Sam shouted. "Pike wins!"

Swenson came over to shake Pike's hand.

"Lousy way to win," Pike said. "I sort of backed into it."

"But you did win," Swenson said. "Congratulations. I've never seen anyone shoot like that."

"Anyone other than you, right?"

Swenson grinned sheepishly. "Right."

"Come on," McConnell said, "one round of drinks is on the house, in honor of the winner."

Pike looked at McConnell, then past him at Bridger, who was approaching.

"You fellas go along," Pike said. "I'll be there."

"All right," McConnell said. He put his arm around young Swenson's shoulders and asked, "Where in hell did you learn to shoot like that?"

Pike moved to meet Bridger.

"What the hell were you doing?" he demanded.

"What do you mean?"

"You missed that shot on purpose."

"What makes you say that?"

"I've never seen you miss that cleanly," Pike said. "You wanted to miss."

"All right," Bridger said. "Since most everyone was

here watching you, I wanted to go over and talk to Hennessy."

"And?"

"He claims he couldn't possibly have gotten out of bed to go and see Fitzsimmons again."

"What else?"

"Well, with the questions I asked, he's got to be suspicious about the way Fitzsimmons died. He might mention his suspicions to somebody."

"If he does, it'll get around camp like a fire through a dry forest. Still, it doesn't matter that much. Sam'll be telling someone about it tonight, and it'll get around soon enough, anyway."

"I suppose."

"Did you believe him?"

"Didn't you?"

"I checked him over," Pike said. "He's got some bad bruises, but all in all I think he was pretty lucky. I think he might have been able to drag himself over there, but I don't know that he would have been able to sneak up on Fitzsimmons."

"Then you don't think he did it."

"I'm inclined to doubt it."

"Well, that leaves everybody else in camp but him."

"Fitz was generally disliked, but I don't think everyone hated him. Why don't we talk to some of the dog soldiers. They're always around camp; maybe one of them saw him arguing with someone."

"That's a good idea, Pike."

"I've got another."

"What?"

"Let's get a drink while it's still free."

"Free?"

"One free round in honor of the winner."

"And who was that?"

Pike looked appalled at the question and said, "Why me, of course."

"The kid almost beat you, huh?"

"He came damn close."

"Sorry I had to drop out," Bridger said, "but to tell you the truth, the way you two were shooting, I think I would have been wasting my time even trying."

"That's a lot of bull."

"Well, let's get that drink so we can wash it down."

They started to walk away together when they both saw Caroline Hennessy standing there, waiting, hands clasped behind her back.

"That's a hell of a fine looking woman," Bridger said.

"I've noticed."

"And I know she ain't standing there waiting for me."

"I wish she'd go tend to her husband."

"Uh huh," Bridger said. "I'll save you a drink."

"Thanks."

They kept walking, but Pike stopped when Caroline stepped in front of him. Bridger kept on as if he hadn't noticed.

"Caroline—"

"I want to congratulate you."

"Well, I appreciate that—"

"No, not here," she said. "In your tent."

"Caroline—"

"Tonight."

"That's not a good idea."

"I don't care," she said. "I'll be at your tent tonight, when everyone is bedded down."

"I won't be there."

"Yes," she said, "you will," and turned on her heels and walked away.

Part Four

CAROLINE

Sixteen

Pike finally did get to the saloon tent in time for his free drink, and then he had a few more with McConnell, Swenson and some others. He did not see Whiskey Sam or Jim Bridger and wondered if they were out doing what he should have been doing, trying to find out who killed Dan Fitzsimmons.

He turned to say something to McConnell and found that his friend was gone. He looked around the tent for him and saw him talking to one of the girls that the owner of the tent had brought with him.

Caroline had been right about one thing. At rendezvous—or any time—a white woman would do very well for herself, because most of the men had been laying with squaws for months. The man who owned this tent had been smart enough to bring some white women with him this year, and McConnell looked like he was discussing price—either that or the size of his penis. Either way, Pike was sure his friend would be busy tonight. That would keep him out of his tent, and probably embarrass Caroline when she went looking for him.

A little later McConnell was back, but only long enough to say, "Don't wait up for me tonight, pal."

"What do you mean?"

"I have an appointment with a lady."

"Do you want me to stay away from the tent?"

"I won't be using our tent," McConnell said. "She has her own, out back." He laughed. "She says it's cozy."

"Wait a minute," Pike said. If McConnell wasn't going to be around that night, that meant he'd be alone in his tent when Caroline came. "You can't—

He stopped when he felt a heavy hand on his shoulder. He looked up and saw Bridger.

"Sam and I have set up a meeting for tonight."

"Where?"

"Right in here, in about a half an hour."

"You're going to close this place down for the meeting?"

"You're not watching the time, my friend," Bridger said. "This place closes in twenty minutes."

Forty minutes later, Whiskey Sam and Jim Bridger were conducting a meeting. In attendance were Pike, McConnell, Rocky Victor, Jim Cooper and some of the other more prominent members of mountain man society. All the merchants who were in camp attended—including Arthur Hennessy, who limped in with the aid of a stout tree branch as a cane. Also there were representatives from the three large fur companies who had sent people to rendezvous to deal with the trappers.

Pike thought Sam did very well in explaining that Dan Fitzsimmons had been killed by person or persons unknown, but that he and Jim Bridger would be looking into it.

"Where's the body?" someone asked. He was one of the fur company men.

"It's in a shallow grave," Sam said.

"Any law been sent for?"

"We'll be sending a man out in the morning."

"What's the holdup?" someone else asked.

Bridger smiled and said, "We're having trouble finding a volunteer. Anyone here want to go?"

No one answered.

"Who do you think done it?" a man called out. He was one of the merchants, a man who sold and repaired guns. Pike didn't remember his name.

"We don't know—" Sam said, but he was interrupted.

"Hell, we do!" a voice yelled.

Pike looked over and saw that the speaker was Packy Weaver, a man he didn't like and who didn't like him. With Packy were is usual partners, Stan Rider and Patch Morton—who did *not* wear a patch. All three were lower than a snake, as far as Pike was concerned.

"What do you mean?" Sam asked.

Packy stood up, happy to be in the spotlight. Like most mountain men, he had some size to him, and some mean—but not as much as Fitzsimmons. He was the kind of man who would never face Pike in a hand to hand fight without Rider and Morton to back him up. In a way, that made him even more dangerous than Fitzsimmons.

"Everybody knows how Pike and Fitzsimmons got along. Everybody knows they had a helluva a fight over a woman that same day that Fitz was killed. You mean to tell me you don't think Pike did it?"

A buzz went through the tent then as men discussed this revelation with whomever was next to them.

If Pike hadn't had so many drinks, he probably wouldn't

have done what he did, but he stood up and shouted at Packy Weaver.

"You wanna step outside, Packy, and see what kind of beating I could've given to Fitz?"

"You gonna kill me too, Pike?" Packy said, sneering. "Sneak up on me and stab me in the back?"

"Why you—" Pike said, making a move toward Weaver, but McConnell and Cooper both grabbed him.

"Easy," McConnell said, "this doesn't look good."

Pike immediately knew that his friend was right, and he was angry with himself. He sat down and berated himself.

The meeting went on for a good twenty minutes, with everybody shouting suggestions, but it finally ended with Sam and Bridger saying that they'd do their best to bring the killer to justice.

"Even if it's Pike?" Packy Weaver shouted.

"No matter who it is," Bridger said firmly.

As the meeting ended and everyone filed out, Weaver was heard to say, "A drunk and Pike's friend, sure they'll find the killer."

"What was that all about?" Bridger asked Pike.

"I made a mistake," Pike said quietly.

"You sure did," Bridger said.

"Nothing better happen to Weaver tonight," Sam said.

"What does that mean?" Pike demanded.

"Easy," Sam said, backing away, "I was making a joke."

Pike stood up and said to Sam, "I'm sorry, Sam. Guess I'm a little tired. I think I'll turn in."

"Want me to come along?" McConnell asked.

"No," Pike said. "You've got a previous engagement, remember?"

"I remember," McConnell said, "but—"

"I'll see you in the morning."

Still very angry with himself, Pike stormed back to his tent. Yanking off his boots, he found himself hoping that Caroline Hennessy *would* come—married or no.

He needed to blow off some steam, and poking her was as good a way as any.

Seventeen

Pike was in his cot when the flap to his tent was opened and Caroline Hennessy stepped in. She had a blanket wrapped around her to ward off the cold.

"Caroline . . ." he said. He sat up and swung his feet to the ground. He was bare-chested and wore only a brief pair of underwear. The wood burner McConnell had gotten for them made for comfortable nights.

"My God," she said, "it's warm in here."

"Yes, it is."

"I guess I don't need this," she said, dropping the blanket to the ground, "do I?"

He couldn't speak. Under the blanket she had been totally naked. Her breasts were large and pear-shaped, topped with dark, chocolate-colored nipples. She was a big woman, with wide hips and heavy thighs.

"Caroline, listen—"

"Pike, if you don't make love to me," she said softly, "I will scream."

He stared at her for a few moments, then decided that she meant what she said. She was just crazy enough to scream her head off and bring the whole camp down on them. In the time since the meeting, his anger had dimmed, but suddenly he was angry all over again.

"All right," he said.

He stood and dropped his underwear. His huge erection sprang free as he lowered his shorts, and she stared at it, fascinated.

He reached for her and pulled her into the circle of his arms. He held her there, and she reached between them with both hands to take hold of his cock.

He kissed her, and as he allowed her searching tongue to enter his mouth, she began to move her hands, stroking him, tugging at him. She writhed against him, and his hands slid from her back to cup her big, cushiony buttocks. He could feel her large, solid breasts pressing against him, the nipples large and tight, poking little holes in his flesh. Her flesh went cold against him, but she was quickly warming up.

She moaned into his mouth, and he quickly swept her up off the floor, amazed at how light she seemed. Her mouth stayed on his, then moved to his neck as they reached the cot.

It only took a moment for them to decide the best way to do it, and they finally agreed that the cot was useless. Reluctantly—because she felt so *good* in his arms—he put her down. Together they pulled the blanket from the cot and spread it on the floor of the tent.

She sat on it first, her legs bent at the knees, gazing at him seductively.

"Come to me, Pike," she said, stretching her arms out, a move that pulled her breasts taut. "I want you to make love to me all night."

He didn't know if he could make love to her all night, but he knew he wouldn't mind trying.

He sat on the blanket next to her and kissed her again, pushing his tongue into her mouth this time. She chewed on him gently, but insistently, her hands roaming over his body. He was hard, she thought, touching his pectorals, his biceps, reaching lower and grabbing his cock. He's so *hard.*

Pike's hand moved over her body, and he found her extremely smooth and full, yet firm.

He went on to search with his mouth.

He chewed her nipples, sucked them, then ran his tongue over her breasts, between them. He kissed her again before moving lower, searching, leaving a wet trail over her belly until he entered the forest of her pubic hair. He could smell her, a sharp, heady odor that excited him. He tasted her, gently at first, then probed with his tongue. He loved doing this to women and never found two women who tasted the same. Yet they were all delicious.

When her time came, she bit her lip to keep from crying out as she lifted her hips, pushing herself harder against his face as he licked and sucked at her. She didn't want anyone outside to hear and come looking.

The first time he entered her, she wanted to be on top. She knew that the hard, unyielding floor would aid penetration, and she wanted as much of his glorious cock inside of her as she could take—and then more.

"Oh, Jesus," she said hoarsely as she lowered herself onto him.

Pike slid into her easily as she lowered her hot, steamy core over him, taking him in inch by inch until he was convinced that he wouldn't be able to go any farther . . . and she took more!

"Oh yes, Pike, my God, yes," she moaned. She started

grinding herself down on him so that her bush mingled with his, and then she threw her head back and simply sat still.

"Caroline—" he said, reaching for her hips.

"No." She pushed his hand away. "I want to savor this, Pike; I want it to go on forever. It's incredible, but it feels as if you are here," she said, touching the space between her breasts, "all the way up here.

"Enjoy it, then . . ." he said, content to wait because she was so warm and wet.

Finally, though, she began to move, slowly at first, as if trying to find the right place, the right tempo. Finally she began to ride him up and down, bracing her hands against his hard stomach, saying "Ooof," every time she came down on him, driving him deeply inside of her.

He reached up to touch her breasts, so full, hefting their weight. He squeezed them in his powerful hands, handling them so gently, then touched her nipples, flicking them easily with his thumbs. He reached for her and pulled her down to him so that he could suck her nipples as she rode him.

She allowed that for a little while, moaning and gasping, but finally she had to sit up and concentrate totally on what she was doing, riding up and down, coming down harder . . . and harder . . . biting her lips as she started to come and then grinding down and staying there because she knew he was about to come.

He felt her insides clench, closing over him, and she literally yanked his seed from him. He started to ejaculate powerfully, long spurts that became decreasingly shorter, and still she seemed to be holding him, milking him. He lifted his hips off the floor, raising not only his own weight but hers as well off the floor. . . .

* * *

Later, when he entered her again, this time with him on top, he grabbed her buttocks and began to slam into her brutally. He knew that his weight must be crushing her, but she never complained once. She wrapped her arms and legs around him, grunting every time he slammed into her but keeping her noise down to a minimum, as he had done. The last thing they wanted was to be interrupted.

Eighteen

There was talk also, that night, during the periods when they rested.

"Won't your husband be looking for you?" he asked. "My God, didn't he see you leave the tent . . . naked? Won't he be waiting for you?"

"Relax," she told him, making little circles on his chest with her hands. "Arthur and I don't have sex very much, Pike. He's not very good at it, and as I think you know now, I am. I need it, and I need it with a man like you."

"But—"

"He won't be waiting for me. He's still sleeping off that beating Fitzsimmons gave him." She kissed his right nipple. "Turns out that's the best thing that could have happened for us."

Pike waited to see if the guilt at having another man's wife would come, but the sex had been so wonderful that it simply never did.

"Do you have a wife . . . somewhere?" she asked.

"No."

"Why not?"

"Never had the urge, I guess."

"But you have known many women. You give too much pleasure not to have known and pleasured many women."

"I've known a few."

She raised herself up on one elbow and looked down at him. "I know I said I wanted to make love all night, but I can't stay. I've got to get back to my tent before anyone wakes up."

"I know," he said. He reached up and ran his forefinger around her right nipple, not touching it. She closed her eyes and bit her bottom lip. She moaned, a sound that made his penis twitch.

"I will come to you here every night of rendezvous."

"That could be risky for you."

"Some things are worth a lot of risk," she said. She slid her hand down over his belly until she had his semi-erect cock in her hand. She ran her thumb over the head, and the entire length of him began to fill with blood, swelling, growing.

"You are right about that," he said, reaching for her.

"No, not like this," she said, moving away from him. He watched as she turned her back and got down on all fours. She raised her big butt in the air and wiggled it. "Like this, Pike. Once more before I leave."

Pike moved in behind her, took hold of her hips, and slid his cock between her thighs and up into the wet, waiting part of her.

She reminded Pike of a wild, untamed animal. Her long black hair matted to her sweaty forehead and neck, her eagerness and sureness, even the very scent of her was wild, filling his nostrils, adding to the excitement that the touch and taste of her had already caused.

This was one hell of a way to let off steam.

* * *

In a small tent behind the saloon tent, Skins McConnell was enjoying the talents of a blond girl named Glory. For a nominal fee, she was perfectly willing to sit astride his rigid cock as long as he wanted her to, leaning over so that he could suck the pink nipples of her plump breasts. Glory's skin was as fair as it could be, which was quite a change from the dark skin of some of the Crow squaws McConnell had had sex with over the past months. And her hair! The pale patch between her legs was ample proof that she was a natural blonde, which made her even more appealing to him.

"I don't suppose I'd be able to reserve you for the rest of rendezvous," he asked in the morning, as he dressed to leave.

She smiled at him, lying on her cot still naked, her right breast so ample—as was the left, of course—that it spilled over her arm.

"There are other men here, you know," she said, "but nobody could stop you from coming into the saloon each night, if you was that interested."

"I am."

"And if I'm available."

"I hope so."

Her smile widened, and she said, "So am I. You're not as big as most of these mountain men—I mean, not as tall or as heavy," she hurriedly added. "And I ain't exactly a big girl, if you know what I mean."

"You mean not tall."

"Right."

She was, if anything, barely five feet tall, which made the fullness of her body seen even more so. She was the direct opposite of Caroline Hennessy, except that Caroline's skin was also fair.

"I'll see you tonight, then," McConnell said.

"I'll look forward to it," she said, cupping one breast in her hand and holding it out to him.

He left, under no illusion as to why she would look forward to it. Number one, he way paying, and number two, maybe he wasn't as big and heavy, or as sloppy, as some of the old timers up here.

As he approached his tent, he wondered idly if Pike was alone or not. At that moment, he saw the tent flap flip open, and Caroline Hennessy—with a blanket wrapped around her—fairly sneaked from the interior and hurried toward her own tent.

Trouble, he thought, looking after her, that woman is trouble. Pike was a big boy, though, and he could certainly take care of himself . . . under most circumstances.

Pike was still awake when McConnell entered the tent, but he made no attempt to let his friend know. In fact, he had just barely gotten the blanket up off the floor and onto the cot when McConnell entered.

Eyes closed, Pike lay still and once again waited for the guilt to come. It never did.

He wondered if this meant that he was becoming an even more hardened person than people already thought he was?

Caroline Hennessy entered the main tent of Hennessy's General Store and dropped the blanket to the floor. Hurriedly she dressed, and then went into the back to check on Arthur. He was fast asleep, and she moved to the second cot in the room and laid down on it, fully clothed.

On one hand she was still terribly excited by the hours she had spent with Pike. It had been a long time since she'd been with such a man—if she had ever been. Maybe it had just been a long time since she'd been with a *real* man, which is probably why she had made that error in judgement with Fitzsimmons.

On the other hand, she was dead tired and knew she'd have to get up soon to open the store.

Maybe Arthur would get back on his feet today.

She closed her eyes, still able to feel Pike's hands on her flesh, her lips. She squeezed her thighs together, feeling herself growing moist.

She looked over at Arthur, who hadn't moved since she had entered.

Did she dare go back to Pike's tent now?

No, there was always tonight.

Arthur Hennessy was awake as Caroline got into her cot, just as he had been awake when she left. Now, as then, he made no attempt to make her aware of that fact.

She had been with Pike, and he damn well knew it.

Well, she and Pike were both going to be in for a hell of a surprise.

Arthur Hennessy was tired of being a nice man.

Nineteen

When Caroline Hennessy woke the next morning, she was surprised to find Arthur at the counter, conducting another inventory.

"You did an inventory when we arrived, Arthur," she said, reminding him.

"I . . . want . . . to . . . know . . . what . . . you . . . sold . . . while . . . I . . . was . . . incapacitated." He spoke very precisely without looking up at her as he wrote in a book.

"I kept a record," she said, exasperated.

He looked up at her, then back down at what he was doing. "I'm just double checking."

"I see you're feeling better today."

"Some," he said.

She nodded, noting that he was apparently back to normal. She started into the back when he asked, "Where did you go last night?"

"What?" she asked, stopping short.

"Last night," he said, still not looking up. "Where did you go?"

"I couldn't sleep," she said. "I went for a walk."

"You were out quite late, weren't you?"

"Yes," she said, turning to face him. "Arthur, I do wish you'd look at me when you talk to me."

"Hmm?" he said. "I'm very busy now, dear. We can talk later, all right?"

She waited to see if he would say anything else, and when he didn't, she turned and went into the back to clean up and dress.

She hadn't thought that he'd seen her last night, but he must have awakened sometime during the night and found her gone.

She was going to have to think of something else for tonight.

Arthur Hennessy looked at his wife's retreating form and smiled to himself.

Who did the bitch think she was fooling?

Eric Fleming worked for the North American Fur Company. They were not one of the largest companies in the country—certainly not the equal of the Hudson's Bay Company—but Fleming had thought that the deal he'd made with Dan Fitzsimmons might help to change that.

Now Fitzsimmons was dead, and Fleming was back to square one.

He wondered if Fitzsimmons had had a partner who might know what his source was for all the fur he'd promised. He'd seen enough of the man to know that he certainly didn't have any friends.

And his death certainly proved that he had enemies.

At least one very deadly one.

* * *

When Whiskey Sam woke that morning, he had a raging erection. He nudged his squaw awake, and she sat up with a resigned look on her face. When she pulled his pants down and saw his swollen cock, her eyes widened, and she immediately bent to her task.

Ever since he'd become booshway, Sam felt like a new man—a younger man. He looked down at the squaw's bobbing head and wondered if this was what it was like for powerful men every morning of their lives.

He felt a rush in his loins and reached for the squaw's head to hold it in place as he filled her mouth.

"Yes!" he cried out as he experienced the most powerful orgasm he'd had in many years.

Jim Bridger woke that morning wondering what the hell he was doing trying to play detective. He was a lot of things—mountain man, trapper, scout—but he certainly wasn't a detective.

Last night he and Whiskey Sam had finally gotten someone to agree to ride for the law; but the round trip would take at least ten days, and by then rendezvous would be over. What they intended to do was find the killer and, even after rendezvous was over, wait for the law to come and pick him up.

First, though, they had to catch him . . . and how the hell was he supposed to do that?

The news that Dan Fitzsimmons had been murdered swept through rendezvous like wildfire. By ten A.M. everyone in camp knew it, and by ten-thirty they were all casting certain looks Pike's way.

"It's started," McConnell said, as he and Pike walked to the chow tent for breakfast.

"I noticed."

"How did it go last night?" McConnell asked.

"I might ask you the same question."

"It went very well."

"Yes," Pike said, "it did."

"Do you intend to see her again?"

"I could ask you—"

"Mine isn't married."

Pike hesitated, then said, "Good point."

"Well?"

"Well what?"

"Are you gonna see her again?"

"I don't know."

"Jesus," McConnell said, "as if you don't have enough problems."

"Like what?"

"Half the people here probably think you killed Fitzsimmons, and the other half are wondering if you did. If she's seen coming from your tent in the middle of the night—"

"Early morning."

"—*or* early morning hours—the woman you fought with Fitzsimmons over—how's that going to look?"

Pike stopped walking and put his hand on his friend's arm.

"I'll tell you something, Skins," he said. "I don't care what people think because I know I didn't kill Fitz."

"And so do I."

"So that makes two of us," Pike said. "Who else do we need?"

He started walking and then looked back to see if McConnell was following. He wasn't.

"Are you going to have breakfast?"

McConnell stared at his friend, then shook his head helplessly and followed.

Twenty

That day there was to be a wrestling contest. The man who usually won was named Solomon Fine. He was a great brute of a man, six-foot-four, almost three hundred pounds, with great sloping shoulders and arms that were corded with great slabs of muscles.

Everyone knew he won every year, and yet every year he had takers.

Of course, the competition was done in a sort of round robin fashion, until they worked their way down to the final two wrestlers, but everyone knew that one of the last two would be Solomon. The competition was really to see who would be the one to face Solomon—and lose—in the final match.

"Are you wrestling this year?" McConnell asked Pike as the combatants gathered around for the start of the competition.

"No, not me," Pike said. "That one time was enough. I don't have to be humbled twice."

Six years ago Pike had decided to try Solomon, and he had held his own for about five minutes. It was a humbling experience for a man of Pike's size and strength.

"Besides," Pike added, "I've had enough fights this week to last me a long time."

"That's just as well," McConnell said.

"Why?"

"If you and Solomon were competing, everyone else would be in it for third place."

"There are some pretty big fellas here."

"There are every year."

"Hey, look."

McConnell looked where Pike was pointing and saw the young man, Swenson, stripping to the waist.

"I guess the kid is wrestling," McConnell said.

"He doesn't look bad."

"He's skinny," McConnell said. "Solomon will break him in half—if he even gets that far."

"Let's go and see who he's wrestling."

They moved closer to the action and saw that the first bout of the day was to be between Swenson and a man named Mel Bolan. Bolan was a big man, over six feet tall and a solid two hundred and twenty pounds.

"What do you think Swenson weighs?" McConnell asked.

"About one ninety," Pike said. He watched the kid and liked the way he moved, light on his feet.

"Bolan will pin him in a minute."

"Want to bet?"

McConnell looked at Pike and said, "A dollar?"

"Big spender," Pike said. "Let's make it two, or when I win all you'll lose is the dollar you won from Whiskey Sam. This way you lose one of your own, too."

"Give me two minutes, and it's a bet," McConnell said.

"What happened to one minute?"

"Two dollars," McConnell said, "two minutes."

"All right, two dollars."

They watched as the two men entered a circle that had been drawn in the dirt. That circle was merely a starting point, because the men could end up wherever they happened to be when one of them was pinned.

As Swenson and Bolan clashed, Pike saw McConnell start counting and knew that his friend would let him know when he reached a hundred and twenty, signifying two minutes.

After the first exchange, Pike knew he'd win. Swenson was much faster than Bolan and seemed to know exactly what he was doing. Bolan grabbed for Swenson, and Swenson ended up behind the bigger man, with Bolan's arm pinned behind him. From there Swenson used one of his legs to sweep Bolan's out from under him, sand then went down with Swenson on top.

Bolan was pinned, and it hadn't taken Swenson two minutes.

"Two dollars," Pike said.

"I don't believe it," McConnell said, handing over the money.

"Believe it," Pike said, "that kid knew exactly what he was doing."

There were several other bouts before Whiskey Sam called for a break. As yet Solomon had not wrestled.

During the break Pike and McConnell approached Hal Swenson.

"That was pretty slick, kid," Pike said.

"Thanks."

"Where did you learn to wrestle?" McConnell asked.

"Back East."

"You're gonna have to face Solomon, you know."

"Who's Solomon?"

"That's Solomon," Pike said, inclining his chin in the big man's direction.

Swenson looked at Solomon and saw a huge man, stripped to the waist, covered with hair and muscle. Solomon was stretching himself out, loosening up his muscles—or trying to. Pike had muscles himself, and he knew how hard it was to stretch them. It was more likely that the kid would get loose with his rangy build.

"He looks like he was cut out of stone," he said.

"That's Solomon," McConnell said.

"He's going to make some noise when he goes down."

McConnell stared at Swenson. "You think you can beat Solomon?"

"Well, I haven't seen him wrestle yet, but if he intended to rely on brute strength, yes, I think I can beat him."

"Brute strength?" McConnell asked. "What else does he need?"

"Well, leverage would help," Swenson said. "And a knowledge of wrestling holds."

"Leverage?" McConnell scoffed. "You'd do better to wrestle Solomon with a big switch, son."

Swenson laughed confidently. "We'll see. I'm going to get closer so I can watch him wrestle when the break's over."

"Sure," Pike said.

"Take a good long look!" McConnell called out. "That kid's crazy."

"I don't think so."

"You wanna bet?"

Pike smiled. "I'll bet you two dollars that the kid makes it all the way to Solomon, and another two that he beats him."

"That's crazy," McConnell said. "You're throwing away your money."

"If the kid makes it all the way through, you'll lose two dollars," Pike said. "When he wrestles Solomon, you'll have a chance to get even."

"Uh uh," McConnell said. "I'll want a chance to get ahead."

"All right," Pike said. "Two dollars the kid makes it to the final two, and then we'll see after that."

"You got a bet."

"Why do you two have your heads so close together?" Whiskey Sam asked, coming up behind them.

Pike looked at Sam and noticed something different.

"Why do you look so chipper," Pike said, "and did you shave? Sam shaved!"

"I don't believe it," McConnell said. "Let me touch it. Ooh, it's baby smooth."

"Get yer hands off my face!" Sam yelled, slapping his hand away. "Is there a law against a man shaving? What are you two cooking up?"

"We're betting," McConnell said, and explained the bet.

"I'll pass on the first part," Sam said, "but if it comes down to the kid and Solomon, I'll want a piece."

"You'll get it," Pike promised. "And send your friends over. I think this kid is going to make me rich."

"You're dreaming," McConnell said as Sam went to restart the competition.

"Next up," Sam shouted, "Solomon!"

He didn't even bother to name Solomon's opponent, and a cheer went up for the big man.

Solomon's opponent was a solidly built man named Frank Grange. As Grange and Solomon stood opposite each other, there was some good-natured ribbing from the crowd.

"Don't hurt him none, Grange."

"Put him down easy, Grange."

Grange acknowledged the crowd with some good-natured nodding and waving of his own.

Twenty seconds later he was down on the ground, pinned.

"Solomon wins!" Whiskey Sam shouted.

When Solomon rose, three men came forward to help up the dazed Grange, who had no knowledge of how he came to be on the ground. Solomon approached him to make sure he was all right, then walked away to the shouts and cheers of the crowd.

McConnell found his way to Hal Swenson's side and said, "Still think you can beat him?"

Swenson smiled. "Brute force is no match for leverage. I'll beat him, all right."

McConnell walked away, shaking his head.

"What's the matter with you?" Pike asked.

"The kid is crazy.

Pike smiled and said, "I'm going to be a rich man."

Part Five

INVESTIGATION

Twenty-One

In the afternoon business began.

The fur companies who had sent representatives—North American, Hudson's Bay and some others—held court in their tents, entertaining or making offers for furs and pelts. Of course, no self-respecting mountain man would sell his skins until he had spoken to all the parties involved.

Bridger and Pike came up with the same idea, that this would be a good time to question the reps about Fitzsimmons. Pike found out about it when the Hudson's Bay representative called him on it.

"Pike, what's with all the questions about Fitzsimmons?"

"Just making conversation, Mike."

Mike Boone was the man Hudson's usually sent, and Pike didn't really think he killed Fitz—even though it was known that the two didn't get along. Boone rarely made an offer on anything Fitzsimmons had to offer. That might have been one of the reasons that Pike liked the thirty-five-year-old rep who looked like he should be a boxer rather than a representative of Hudson's Bay.

"Like Bridger?"

"What about Bridger?"

"He was asking about Fitz, too."

"What was he asking?"

"What I was doing the night Fitz got himself killed," Boone said. "Pretty subtle, huh?"

"Bridger's no detective."

"And neither are you."

"Have you heard who the popular choice is for the killer?"

"Who hasn't? You."

"Think I did it?"

"No."

"What would you do if everyone suspected you?"

Boone nodded. "I'd go around asking a lot of fool questions."

"May I?"

"Be my guest."

Pike sat down. "Did you have any dealings with him?"

"I don't buy from Fitz, you know that."

"Who was buying from him?"

"I can't say for sure; but I've seen him with the guy from North American a couple of times, and I saw him coming out of the North American tent that night."

"The night he was killed?"

"Uh huh."

"Have you told anyone else?"

"No."

"Not even Bridger?"

"We didn't get that far."

"What's the rep's name from North American?"

"Uh, Fleming, Eric Fleming."

"What kind of guy is he?"

"The kind of guy who would work for North American."

"Ah," Pike said, "trustworthy, loyal—"

"—and as crooked as a snake."

"And he was dealing with Fitz."

"I said he was talking to him. Whether or not he was dealing with him, you're gonna have to ask him."

"I think I will," Pike said, "but while we're here let's talk furs. . . .

Packy Weaver sat down opposite Eric Fleming and proceeded to dicker. At one point, Fleming deviated from the negotiation, as he had with everyone.

"Damn shame about Fitzsimmons."

"Yeah," Weaver said. "Look, the price for beaver should be higher. I mean, with them being scarce and all."

"I suppose so," Fleming said. "If you had some beaver pelt—and I mean, in quantity—I could probably do something about the price."

"Yeah?"

"I believe Fitzsimmons had said something about having some pelts."

"He did?" Weaver's eyes acquired a greedy glint—the very glint Fleming had been waiting to catch in someone's eyes.

"I said the same thing to him, about quantity, and he told me he'd have something for me. You wouldn't know what he was talking about, would you?"

Weaver opened his mouth to reply, but as usually happens with greedy men, they somehow get smarter during their periods of greed.

"Well, I might be able to do something," Weaver said. "I'd have to talk to my associates."

"Associates?"

"Rider and Morton."

"I don't know them."

"You don't want to," Weaver said. "You just do your negotiating with me."

"When we have something to negotiate, I will."

"I'll be in touch," Weaver said. He stood and headed for the exit but stopped short when the tent flap was tossed back and Pike walked in.

"I knew I'd find you in here when I saw your two uglies outside," Pike said.

"Keep it up, Pike," Weaver said. "When the law asks for volunteers to hang you for killing Fitz, I'm gonna be first in line."

"You're going to have a long wait."

Weaver laughed and left the tent.

Twenty-Two

"Can I help you?" Fleming asked. "Or should I say, can North American help you?"

"North American can't," Pike said, approaching the table the man was using as a desk, "but you can."

"How do you mean?"

"What were you and Dan Fitzsimmons talking about the night he died?"

"The night he died?" Fleming asked, frowning.

"Come on, Fleming. He was seen coming out of your tent that night."

"Maybe so," Fleming said, "but if he was, I wasn't in the tent at the time. I didn't see him that night."

"You saw him twice before that."

"Maybe I did, but I've seen a lot of people. I suppose he was trying to sell me some furs."

"You suppose? You don't know?"

"I talk to so many people."

"You'd remember him," Pike said. "He was booshway, had a big piece of metal hanging around his neck. You'd remember him, all right."

Fleming frowned, as if he was truly trying to remember.

"I believe I did talk to him, but he didn't like my price,

very much. He was going to try some of the other representatives."

"Like Hudson's Bay?"

"Yes, I believe he was going to speak to Mr. Boone."

"Boone wouldn't have anything to do with Fitzsimmons," Pike said. "He was the kind of man your company would deal with, though."

"What kind of man is that?"

"Underhanded."

"I'm afraid I'm going to have to object to that statement, Mr. . . ."

"Pike."

"Ah, now I understand," Fleming said. "You're the man who beat up Mr. Fitzsimmons."

"It was more like give and take."

"But you gave more than you took."

"That's usually the general idea."

"I was given to understand that you killed him."

Pike leaned on the table with all his weight, and the legs almost buckled. Fleming recoiled from the nearness of the bigger man.

Grinning tightly, Pike said, "I don't generally use a knife." He poked Fleming in the chest with a forefinger like an iron spike and said, "I'd use my hands if I wanted to kill a man."

"I see," Fleming said. He was trying to back away from Pike's finger, but he had no place to go.

Pike removed the finger from the man's chest and stood up.

"I'll give you some time to think things over and try to remember," Pike said. "When you have something to tell me, I'll be around."

Pike left, and Fleming who had holding his breath let it out.

If Weaver and his friends came up with the pelts, he'd do business with them, but he wanted one other thing thrown in.

He didn't like being threatened, and he wanted Pike to find that out.

When Pike came out of the North American Fur tent he did not see Weaver or any of his men. He did, however, see Jim Bridger.

"Bridger!"

Bridger turned and waited for Pike to catch up to him. Pike briefly went over his conversation with Mike Boone and Eric Fleming.

"It would seem that Mr. Fleming has to know something," Bridger said.

"Something that he's not offering us."

Bridger nodded. "Or maybe he killed Fitzsimmons himself."

"Why?"

"That's what we'd have to find out."

"Have you talked to the other representatives?"

"Yes. They seem to feel the same way about Fitzsimmons that Boone does."

"There's something else to consider."

"What?"

"Packy Weaver was in with Fleming for a long time."

"Weaver? Isn't he the one who hangs around with those other two . . . what are their names?"

"Rider and Morton, yeah, that's him."

"What was his relationship with Fitzsimmons?"

"I don't think he had one, but I could be wrong."

"Maybe I should have a talk with Weaver and his friends," Bridger suggested.

"You might get more from him than I would. We don't get along real well."

"Well, I've never had any dealings with him one way or the other, so we'll see what happens. I guess it's a good thing you talked to Boone. You and he are friendly?"

"Some."

"He sure didn't tell me as much as he told you."

Pike simply shrugged at that and said, "Then again, you aren't suspected of murder by most of the people here, like I seem to be."

'Maybe we can do something about that."

"Who did you and Sam send for the law?"

"Bill Flint."

"Good man."

"Couldn't get a volunteer," Bridger said. "Nobody thought enough of Fitzsimmons to miss rendezvous on his account."

"How did you get Flint to go?"

"We told him that it would help you," Bridger said. "That seemed to do it. You seem to have a lot of people in camp who *don't* think you killed Fitzsimmons, Pike. I thought you ought to know that."

"Thanks," Pike said. "It helps some."

"Well, I'd better find Weaver before he and his boys can cook up a story of some kind. See you later."

"I'll buy you a drink."

Bridger nodded and left. Pike stood there for a few moments trying to think of what his next move should be. Unfortunately, all he could think to do was go and see Caroline Hennessy, and he didn't really want to do that.

Well, he *did* want to do it, actually, which was precisely why he decided not to go.

He decided to go and watch some more of the wrestling competition instead.

Twenty-Three

Bridger found Weaver walking around without his two friends and approached him.

"Weaver, can I talk to you for a minute?"

Weaver turned, and when he saw who it was, he stopped. A nasty smile spread across his face slowly.

"The great Jim Bridger. You never had time for me before, why the change now?"

"I don't know what you're talking about, Weaver—"

"I'm talking about you high and mighty types, you and Pike. They tell stories about you, the others. You fellas are legends, and you never have time for my type.'

"Maybe you should change your type."

"Why? You want to talk to me now, don't ya? What's it about?"

"Fitzsimmons."

"What about him." Wever's eyes narrowed suspiciously.

"I was wondering what you were doing the night he was killed."

"Oh, I get it," Weaver said. "You figure by pointing a finger at me you'll get your friend Pike off the hook. What's the matter; things starting to look bad for him?"

"I'm just asking questions, Weaver, of you and a lot of people."

"Well, I don't know nothin'. I wasn't friends with Fitzsimmons, and I don't know nothin' about his death."

"What about your buddies, Rider and Morton?"

"Stan and Patch speak for themselves, but just between you and me, they don't know nothin' either. You ask them, though. Satisfy your curiosity."

"I intend to."

"You ain't gettin' your friend off of this one, Bridger. He's the only one who had cause to kill Fitzsimmons."

"What cause?"

"They was both after the same woman, wasn't they?"

"You think a woman is reason for murder?"

"People been killed for a lot less than that, Bridger. You should know that. I got things to do. Sorry I couldn't help you."

Weaver turned and walked away. His tone of voice said he wasn't sorry at all.

Both Swenson and Solomon wrestled twice more that day and won both bouts easily. As Pike and McConnell headed for the saloon tent, McConnell was still unconvinced about Swenson.

"I know the kid has looked good," he said, "but Jesus, he only weighs one-ninety soaking wet. How can he expect to beat Solomon?"

"He's told you how, Skins," Pike said.

"Yeah, leverage, he keeps saying leverage. You gotta do a lot more to Solomon than trip him in order to beat him."

"You want to increase the bet?"

McConnell thought a moment and said, "No. I'm starting to think that he will end up wrestling Solomon. Let's wait until then to talk about the bet."

"Okay."

"Let's get that drink."

On the way to the saloon tent, Pike caught a glimpse of Weaver with Rider and Morton. He wondered if Bridger had gotten to any of them yet, because they sure as hell had their heads together now. Whatever story they were thinking up, they'd all stick to it from now until hell froze over.

"Something was going on between Fitzsimmons and that feller from North American, Fleming," Weaver said to Rider and Morton.

"Like what?" Rider asked.

"I don't know, but I think it had something to do with beaver pelts."

"Beaver is mighty scarce these days, Packy," Morton said.

"I know that," Weaver said impatiently. "What if Fitzsimmons found himself a source, though. Someplace where he thought he could get a lot of beaver? That'd be worth something to this Fleming fella."

"So what' that to us?" Morton asked.

"Stupid, Patch," Weaver said, shaking his head. "Are you always gonna be stupid? If we can find out where Fitzsimmons was gonna get his beaver, we could make our own deal with Fleming. This could mean a lot of money for us."

"How are we gonna find out, though?" Rider asked. "Fitzsimmons is dead."

"But his tent is still there," Weaver said. "Tonight,

we're gonna see what he had in his tent just before he died."

"You think maybe he wrote something down?" Rider asked.

"Maybe."

"I can't read, Weaver," Rider said.

"Me neither," Morton said.

"Well lucky for you two morons, I can. Jesus," he said, shaking his head, "I don't even know why I'm cuttin' you guys in on this."

"We been friends for a long time, Packy," Morton said.

"Partners, maybe," Weaver said, "but not friends. Still, sometimes that's better, ain't it? I think a man's more likely to turn on a friend than a partner. Don't you think so?"

"Whatever you say, Packy," Morton said.

"You fellas would never turn on me, would you?"

"Never," Rider said, exchanging nervous looks with Morton. Both men knew that if they ever did turn on Weaver, he'd kill them in a second.

Weaver smiled. "See what I mean?"

In the saloon tent Pike kept his word and bought Bridger a drink. They sat at a barrel while McConnell went over to talk to Solomon. Probably wanted to make sure the champ was feeling all right.

"Did you talk to Weaver?" Pike asked.

"Yeah, but he swore that he didn't know anything about Fitzsimmons, or his murder."

"Unfortunately, I believe him," Pike said.

"Why?"

"Fitz and Weaver were cut from the same cloth. I think

that was the reason they steered clear of each other. I really *don't* think they ever had any dealings. There's just no reason for Weaver to have killed Fitzsimmons."

"Unless he wanted to frame you for it."

"He could have picked somebody else to frame me. Fitz had too many other enemies for the frame to take."

"You don't think it will?"

"Not seriously. Oh, it's an annoyance, all right, to have people you once thought of as friends—sort of—look at you funny, or walk the other way when they see you, but that'll blow over as soon as we find out who really killed Fitz."

"I don't think I'm cut out to be a lawman," Bridger said. "I really don't know where to go from here."

"I think all we can do is continue to ask questions. Sooner or later the killer will get edgy and make a wrong move. All we have to do is be ready to move when he does."

"Well, I'm ready."

"So am I," Pike said, and added, "for another beer. How about you?"

"Sure."

Pike looked around for McConnell and saw that his friend had abandoned Solomon for the charms of the blonde he'd been with the night before. Since McConnell was keeping her occupied, Pike decided to get up and get the drinks himself.

Waiting at the bar, Pike looked around the tent, which was filled almost to capacity. The thing he found odd was that he could see neither Weaver, Rider nor Morton, three men who liked to drink and usually spent a lot of time in the saloon.

When he had seen them last, they had looked like they were planning something. He wondered now, as he walked back to Bridger with the beer, what they were up to.

Twenty-Four

"What's the matter?" Bridger asked Pike.

"I don't see Weaver or his friends."

"Why should you?"

"They're always in here at night drinking too much," Pike said. "Why not tonight?"

"Okay, I give up. Why not?"

"I don't know," Pike said, standing up, "but I'm going to find out."

"Wait," Bridger said, "I'll come with you."

"Why can't I come in, too?" Rider wanted to know.

"Because we need someone to stand watch out here," Weaver explained.

"So, why can't Morton?"

"Because I'm telling you."

"Can't you ever do what you're told?" Morton asked.

"Why don't you shut up?" Rider said. "I'm talking to Weaver."

"Just do what he says!" Morton argued.

"You never do what you're told!"

"I always do what I'm told!"

"Will both of you shut up!" Weaver hissed. "You're going to bring the whole camp down on us."

Rider and Morton both fell into a resentful silence.

"Now, Rider, you stay out here and keep watch."

Rider nodded.

"Morton, come inside."

Morton nodded, then made a face at Rider and followed Weaver into the tent.

"What are we looking for?" Morton asked.

"Nothing, if you don't keep your damn voice low."

Morton asked the same question in a lower voice.

"Anything that looks like it's about beaver pelts," Weaver said.

"Weaver, you know I can't read—"

"Just call me if something looks interesting," Weaver said, impatiently. He should have left Morton outside with Rider.

After a few moments—and after Morton had bothered him three times to look at nothing—he said, "All right, damn it, go outside and help Rider keep watch. I'll be out in a little while."

"Why—"

"Because you're no damn help, that's why!" Weaver said. "Now go!"

Grudgingly, Morton went outside.

"I knew it," Pike said.

"What are they looking for?" Bridger asked.

"I don't know, but I'd like to find out."

"Then why don't we?" Bridger said.

Pike looked at Rider, who was standing watch, then looked at Bridger and said, "Yeah, why don't we?"

Morton stood outside and looked around, but he couldn't see Rider anywhere.

"Where the hell—" he began.

He was about to go inside and tell Weaver when a hand the size of a bear's paw closed around his mouth and pulled his head back until he thought his neck would snap.

Weaver was bent over, examining the contents of one of Fitzsimmons' hunting pouches, when he heard someone enter the tent behind him.

"Damn it, I told you morons to wait for me outside. You're supposed to be on watch."

"They were," Pike said.

Weaver spun around, his hand moving for the pistol in his belt, but he froze when he saw both Pike and Bridger. Their hands were empty, but he knew it would be foolhardy to kill one of them.

"What's going on?" Weaver asked.

"That's what we were going to ask you," Pike said. "Where are Rider and Morton?"

"They're both having a nap."

"Are they dead?"

"What do you care?" Bridger asked.

"Let me by," Weaver said, starting toward them, trying to get between them.

Pike stiff-armed him, and Weaver staggered backward, backpedalling to try and keep his balance. The back of his knees struck something, and he fell over it and onto his ass.

"Stay down, Weaver," Pike said, "and answer some questions."

"I don't have to answer anything."

"What were you looking for in here?"

"Nothing."

"Wrong answer," Bridger said.

"Don't make us ask again," Pike added.

"You two living legends aren't going to get anything out of me."

"Oh yes we are," Pike said. "It may not be what we want, but it sure as hell isn't going to be anything you want."

"What are you talking about?"

Pike stared at him. "Blood."

Bridger took his knife out and Weaver's eyes widened.

"Now," Pike said, "I'll ask you again . . ."

Later, after they released Weaver and told him to leave rendezvous with Rider and Morton, Bridger said, "Did you believe him?"

"Yes," Pike said. "I don't think he knew what he was looking for, or he wouldn't have made such a mess looking for it."

"What about letting him go?"

"What'd you want to do, kill him?"

"What if he turns out to be the killer?"

"Then I'll have made a mistake."

"I guess we'll have made a mistake," Bridger said, sharing the blame. "Did you believe him about Fleming and Fitzsimmons?"

"Yes."

"I guess that means we talk to Fleming."

Pike looked at Bridger and said, "Oh, yes."

Twenty-Five

Something woke Eric Fleming, and when he looked up from his cot, he saw two huge men standing over him.

"What the hell—"

"Hi," Pike said, "remember me?"

Pike lit a lamp so that Fleming would be able to see his face.

"Pike?"

"That's right," Pike said, "and this is my friend, Jim Bridger."

"What are you doing in my tent in the middle of the night?"

"Oh, we got an urge to ask you a few questions," Bridger said.

"About what?"

"About the night Dan Fitzsimmons was killed."

Fleming looked at Pike. "We talked about this, didn't we?"

Pike smiled. "We're going to talk about it again."

Fleming frowned and said, "Let me get up and—"

As he started to rise, Pike put his hand on the man's chest and pushed him back down.

"Hey!"

"No," Pike said, "don't get up. Stay comfortable."

"This isn't very comfortable—" Fleming complained.

"Tough it out," Bridger said.

Fleming settled back down on his cot with a resigned look. "What do you want to know?"

"Well, for starters," Pike said, "did you kill Fitzsimmons?"

"No!"

"All right, then," Pike said, "what kind of a deal did you have going with him?"

"Who says I had a deal—"

"Weaver," Pike said. "You remember Weaver? You talked to him yesterday."

"I talked to a lot of people yesterday."

"You had just finished talking to him when I walked in," Pike said.

"Oh . . . him."

"You led him to believe that you had a deal going with Fitzsimmons, and that you wouldn't mind making the same deal with him."

"I never said that—"

"I didn't say you said that," Pike said. "I said you led him to believe it."

"I can't help what he believes."

"Let me tell you what he believes," Pike said, "and you can tell me if I'm right or wrong."

Fleming did not reply.

"Fitzsimmons told you that he had access to beaver pelts in abundance, and you lowered your prices to the rest of us in anticipation of the deal. You were going to pay Fitzsimmons a higher price than the rest of us because he had more pelts. It was probably his idea. Pay him more or he'd take them someplace else. Meanwhile, he was getting you to pay the rest of us less just out of pure meanness. How am I doing?"

Fleming sulked a moment, arms folded across his chest, and then said, "All right, yeah. He said if I lowered my offer to the rest of you, he'd sell me all the pelts I wanted."

"Did you ask him why?"

"He just wanted to make sure he got more—a lot more—than the rest of you."

Pike looked at Bridger and said, "That sounds like Fitz, all right . . . the bastard."

Pike looked back at Fleming and said, "And you didn't mind lowering your offer to the rest of us because you knew you'd at least pick up *some* pelts cheap."

Fleming didn't respond.

"All right, so you told Weaver that if he could come up with the pelts, you'd do the same deal."

Fleming nodded. "I figured Fitzsimmons might have a partner, and if it wasn't Weaver, maybe he knew who it was."

"You didn't know Fitzsimmons very well," Pike said. "He wouldn't split his take with anyone."

"Did you kill him?" Bridger asked.

"Why would I kill him?" Fleming said. "We had a deal. I was going to stock up on beaver for my company. That would have meant a bonus for me. I had no motive to kill Fitzsimmons."

Unfortunately, that made a world of sense to both Pike and Bridger.

"As far as I'm concerned," Fleming said, gaining confidence, "you still had the best motive, Pike."

Pike took a step forward, but Bridger put a hand on his arm to stay him.

"Could I get some sleep now?" Fleming asked.

"Sure," Bridger said, "sweet dreams."

He pulled on Pike's arm and led him outside.

"He's right," Bridger said outside, "you still have the best motive."

"I thought we had something here," Pike said. "I didn't expect to come up so empty."

"Well, we're not totally empty," Bridger said as they walked away from Fleming's tent. "We know Fitzsimmons was working a deal with Fleming. Now, what if he did have a partner, and the partner killed him?"

"I doubt that, but okay, let's work on that assumption," Pike said. *If* he had a partner, and *if* the partner killed him, then he'll be getting in touch with Fleming to make his own deal."

"So we need to have someone watch Fleming."

"But all Fleming is going to do all day long is talk to people."

"Then we need for him to try talking to someone in secret," Bridger said.

"All right," Pike said, "I don't think Fitz had a partner, but we'll talk to Whiskey Sam tomorrow about having someone watch Fleming."

"You want to go and have another drink?"

"No," Pike said, "I think I'm going to head for my tent and turn in. I'm not getting any younger."

"Don't remind me," Bridger said. "I'll see you in the morning."

They parted company, and Pike walked to his tent, feeling depressed. When they'd first spotted Weaver and his boys at Fitzsimmons' tent, he really thought they had something.

Now all he had was an empty feeling in his stomach,

and he had maintained the number one spot on the suspects list for Fitzsimmons' murder.

When he entered his tent, he wasn't surprised to find that McConnell wasn't there. He was, however, surprised and—to his profound confusion—disappointed to find that neither was Caroline Hennessy there.

Undressing and starting up the wood burner, he told himself that it was actually better that Caroline was not there. He didn't need another involvement in his life, right now.

Twenty-Six

"I'm glad you weren't busy tonight," McConnell said as he undressed.

Glory was already undressed and waiting for him on a blanket they had spread on the floor.

"To tell you the truth," she said, "I waited for you."

"You did?"

She nodded. "I turned down three men while I was waiting for you."

"Why?"

She shrugged. "I like it better with you," she said. "You're gentle, and you care about my pleasure as well as yours."

"I didn't think—" he started to say, then stopped.

"What?"

"No . . ."

"Go ahead," she said, and then stopped him by saying, "Oh, I see. You didn't think whores felt anything."

"I'm sorry," he said. "I didn't mean to insult—"

"Shut up," she said. She reached for him and took hold of his cock, drawing him to her. "You're right, in a way. We don't always feel something, but with you, I do."

She rose to her knees and slowly worked her tongue up

and down the thick length of him, and then she took him into her mouth as far as she could and began to suck on him as if it were the sweetest piece of candy she had ever had, sliding him in and out, using her other hand to cup his testicles.

When McConnell felt his legs beginning to tremble, he said, "Glory," and reached for her. She released him, and he went to his knees with her.

He kissed her. Her lips were full and firm, sweet tasting, as was her tongue which just flicked out and touched his lips lightly. The second kiss was a little more involved, and with the third their tongues were fencing with each other. He slid his hands down and cupped her firm behind, pulling her closer to him. The heat of her breasts was intense.

Still kissing, they laid down on the blanket together, their legs intertwined, thighs rubbing against each other. The flesh of her body was like her breasts, smooth and hot.

When he began to kiss her breasts she moaned, and when he sucked her nipples she caught her breath.

"Please, Skins, please . . ." she said, and he knew what she wanted.

He mounted her and slid into her easily, gently, until he was firmly set deep inside of her. She spread her legs as much as she could and bit her lower lip as he started pumping, long easy strokes at first, and then harder and faster until she was moaning and clutching at him.

"Yes," she whispered into his ear. Even in the throes of passion, she was aware of their surroundings, and that being too loud could attract attention. She wanted it to be just the two of them, as if there was no one else on earth. "Oh, yes, Skins, yes, it's . . . been . . . too . . . damn . . . long!"

At the moment of her orgasm she reached for his head, turned his mouth to her and kissed him hard, thrusting her tongue into his mouth. When he came, she wrapped her thighs around him and squeezed as hard as she could—which was pretty damn hard for a woman her size.

Caroline Hennessy wanted Pike so badly she was beside herself with it, but she couldn't think of a good excuse to get up and leave the tent.

Arthur Hennessy was lying awake on his cot, making some fool list for the next day. At least if he would go to sleep she might be able to slip out for just a little while.

"Are you going to keep that lamp on all night?" she complained.

"Hmm?" he said. "Oh, no, not all night. I just have to finish this. You go on to sleep, dear."

How could she sleep when every muscle in her body ached to be with Pike?

She turned her back on her husband and waited for the lamp to go out.

After they made love, they talked, which they hadn't done the night before—but then, last night Glory was just a whore he wanted to be with. Tonight, she was a woman he enjoyed being with.

"What's your real name?" he asked.

"Gloria."

He felt that she had deliberately held back her last name, so he didn't ask her about it.

"You're friends with that man Pike, aren't you?" she asked.

"Pike? Sure, we're friends."

"It's a shame about him."

"*What* about him?"

"Killing that other man, Fitzsimmons."

"Pike didn't kill him," McConnell said. "A lot of people just think he did."

"And you don't think so?"

"No, I don't," McConnell said. "It's just going to be hard to change some people's minds with some kind of proof."

"Like what?"

"Like maybe finding someone else who was having a problem with Fitzsimmons."

"Someone else he might have had a fight with?"

"Right."

She pushed herself up on her elbow and said, "I think I might be able to help."

"How?"

"I saw him have a fight with someone."

"You did?" Now he propped himself up on an elbow to face her. "Who?"

"One of those Indians who wear the armbands."

"A dog soldier?"

"Yes."

"Which one?"

Now she looked alarmed as she said, "I don't know which one. I mean . . . they all look alike."

"All right," McConnell said, "just tell me what you saw, Gloria. . . ."

Finally, Caroline Hennessy thought as she listened to her husband's breathing. They had been married long enough for her to be able to tell from the way he was breathing that he was asleep.

As quietly as possible, she slipped from her cot fully dressed—she had told her husband that she was cold—and moved into the front area of the tent. There she pulled on her boots and hurriedly went out into the cold.

She hurried out of need for Pike and out of a need to get out of the cold, but as she came within sight of Pike's tent, she saw a man approaching it. The moon was full, and she could see that it was Pike's friend, Skins McConnell, with whom he shared the tent.

She watched as McConnell entered the tent, wondering why the man wasn't with his whore, as he had been the night before.

She had three choices now. She could go to the tent anyway, she could stand there and wait to see if McConnell was going to leave and risk freezing to death, or she could go back to her own tent.

She waited five minutes, and when the cold started to get to her bones, she turned and went back to her tent.

Twenty-Seven

When McConnell entered the tent he shared with Pike, he shook his friend awake.

"Wha—" Pike said, coming awake badly because he'd only just fallen asleep.

"Whoa, easy," McConnell said, backing away from Pike's strong hands.

"What the hell—" Pike said, wiping his face with his hands. "I feel like I just fell asleep."

"I'm sure you did," Skins said, looking around.

"Stop looking around; she wasn't here," Pike said. "What did you wake me up for?"

"I found out something tonight that I thought you'd want to hear."

"Yeah, well, Bridger and I found out some things as well," Pike said, "but since you thought your news was important enough to wake me up, you go first."

McConnell told Pike what he had learned from Glory, about the dog soldier she had seen Fitzsimmons fighting with.

"Actually, she says it wasn't much of a fight. Fitzsimmons put the dog soldier down easily and then kicked him a few times."

"A dog soldier wouldn't appreciate that."

"He might even dislike it enough to kill Fitzsimmons in his sleep."

"I suppose," Pike said, rubbing his jaw. "Can we find this particular dog soldier?"

"She wasn't able to tell me much about him."

"Would she recognize him if she saw him again?"

"I'm not sure."

"Would she be willing to try and identify him?"

"I could ask her."

"Ask her real nice."

McConnell smiled. "What did you learn?" he asked.

Pike explained about finding Weaver in Fitzsimmons' tent, and then about Fleming and Fitzsimmons.

"You seem fairly certain that neither Weaver nor Fleming killed Fitzsimmons."

"I am," Pike said. "Weaver had no motive, and Fleming certainly had motive to want Fitzsimmons alive."

"If you keep eliminating suspects—"

"I know," Pike said. "Rendezvous still has a couple of days to run. I don't see any reason to leave. It sure wouldn't make me look any more innocent."

"I guess not."

"And even if I did leave, there wouldn't be any reason for you to go along."

"Ah," McConnell said, "it wouldn't be any fun around here without you."

"I'm flattered," Pike said, lying back on his cot. "Are you going back to your Glory?"

"Not tonight," McConnell said. "I can talk to her in the morning."

"Then how about us getting some sleep?" Pike suggested. "In the morning we can start looking for our dog soldier."

"There can't be that many here," McConnell said, undressing, "can there?"

"Ten or twelve, I imagine. You can walk your Glory—"

"Her name is Gloria."

"You can walk her through the camp and see if she recognizes any of them."

McConnell got into his cot. "And if she doesn't?"

"Then we'll just have to question them all," Pike said, "one by one."

The dog soldier watched the moon.

It was full and glowed as if it had a life of its own. The dog soldier liked looking at the moon. It was what he was doing when the booshway—the old booshway, Fitzsimmons—had come along and asked him why he was standing around. The dog soldier had been about to answer when suddenly Fitzsimmons had struck him. This had confused the dog soldier, as he hadn't felt that he'd done anything to deserve being struck. When he tried to say this to Fitzsimmons, he was struck again.

Having been struck twice, the dog soldier did the only thing he could think of—he struck back. The blow hit Fitzsimmons in the face, and while it did little harm, it did serve to enrage him. He pummeled the smaller dog soldier to the ground, and then kicked him while he was down.

Kicked him like a dog—and then spit on him!

The dog soldier lay there after Fitzsimmons had left, and vowed revenge for the cruel treatment. He burned with shame at the treatment he'd received at the hands of the white man. He knew, however, that he would not be able to best the bigger man face-to-face, so he decided that he would have to do it from behind. Having been shamed once, the second shame was necessary.

The dog soldier respected Pike and was sorry that the suspicious eye was falling on him, but there was no way that the dog soldier could confess to killing Fitzsimmons. If he did, everyone would know not only his shame, but his double shame.

What the dog soldier did not know was that allowing another man to pay for his deed would be the worst shame of all.

Part Six

DOG SOLDIERS

Twenty-Eight

The morning brought with it the finale of the wrestling competition.

"Are you gonna watch the wrestling?" McConnell asked Pike at breakfast.

"Yup, and so are you," Pike said. "In fact, bring your friend Gloria."

"Oh, I get it," McConnell said. "Almost everybody will be watching Solomon beat young Swenson."

"You mean, they'll be watching Swenson beat Solomon."

"You don't still believe that, do you?"

"We'll watch today and find out."

After breakfast Pike, McConnell and more than half the people at rendezvous moved over to where the wrestling competition was to take place.

"We have four wrestlers left," Whiskey Sam called out. "Solomon will face Bob Mack, and Swenson will face Will Murphy. The two winners will face each other immediately following the end of the first two matches . . . with no rest period."

"Now what's the idea of that?" McConnell asked.

"I guess they want to be sure the best man wins," Pike said. "The man who's in the best shape, I guess."

"Well, that's Solomon."

"He's not in better shape," Pike said, "he's just bigger."

"We'll see who's in the best shape."

"I'll see who's in the best shape," Pike said. "You'd better go and find your girl."

"Speaking of girls," McConnell said, "there's yours."

Pike looked across the wrestling area and saw Caroline watching him.

"She's not my girl," Pike denied. "She's got a husband."

"Well, you remember that, don't you?"

Pike turned his head and stared at McConnell.

"All right, I'm going," McConnell said reluctantly, "but let me know exactly what happens.

"You'll be the first to know."

Caroline Hennessy kept her eyes on Pike and not on the combatants who were about to lock up.

She'd had a fight with her husband that morning because he wanted her to stay and help him run the store.

"There's a wrestling match going on," she said, "and I want to watch it. You don't need me here."

"Caroline," Arthur Hennessy said, "I don't know what's gotten into you since we got here. You've never acted like this before."

"Maybe," she said, taunting him, "it's seeing all these real men up here."

"You mean like your hero, Pike?"

"Yes, like Pike," she said, "and like the men who are wrestling this morning."

"Never mind the men who are wrestling," Hennessy said. "You want to go out and see Pike. What happened, did he turn you away last night?"

She grinned at Arthur Hennessy then and said, "No man has ever turned me away, Arthur." She left the tent.

She didn't know what would happen when she went back to the tent, but she didn't care. All she wanted to do was work her way through the crowd until she was standing with Pike. Given the choice of having sex with Arthur Hennessy or simply standing next to Pike, she would choose Pike.

And she knew it had nothing to do with love. It had to do with the way she'd felt the other night with him.

She wanted to feel like that again.

By the agreement of all four wrestlers, both matches began at the same time.

Solomon rushed Big Bob Mack and struck him with his shoulder, flattening Mack. Mack was a big man, all right, but he could not match Solomon's bulk. While he was on his back, Solomon dropped all his weight on him, driving the air from the man's body, and then he pinned him. . . .

Will Murphy was roughly the size of Bob Mack, which meant he outweighed young Swenson by a good thirty pounds or so. Seeing the shoulder maneuver that Solomon used to knock Bob Mack down, he tried the same move on Swenson. He charged the younger, slighter man, his shoulder forward; only when he got there, Swenson had stepped aside. Murphy found himself tripping over Swenson's foot and then skidding on his chest. Before he could move, Swenson was sitting on the small of his back with his hands laced beneath Murphy's chin, and rather than have his back or neck broken, Murphy submitted. . . .

To show that there were no hard feelings, Murphy shook hands with Swenson, congratulating him.

"Good luck against Solomon, kid," Murphy said. "You're gonna need it."

"What did I miss?" McConnell asked, coming up on Pike's right.

"You missed the set up of our bet," Pike said. "Solomon against Swenson."

"What are you betting?" Gloria asked.

Pike leaned forward slightly in order to get a look at Gloria. She was short and buxom, and very pretty.

"Well, we hadn't agreed, but—"

"How about five dollars," McConnell suggested.

"It's a good thing we're friends or I'd call you cheap," Pike said. "Gloria, I appreciate you coming here to help."

"I'm glad to do it. What do you want me to do?"

"Just see if you recognize any of these dog soldiers you see standing around."

"I'll try, but I don't really think I can."

"That's all right, just do the best you can, and I'll appreciate it."

"Sure," she said, hugging McConnell's arm.

"Uh oh," McConnell said, looking past Pike.

"What?" Pike asked, but then he felt someone slip an arm into the crook of his left arm, and turned to find Caroline standing there.

"Caroline—"

"Pike, I'm sorry I couldn't come last night."

"We have to talk, Caroline—"

"Later," Caroline said. "They're about to start the match."

Solomon and Swenson squared off, circling each other warily. Apparently, they'd seen enough of each other to have mutual respect.

Both men had finished their first matches so fast that neither had been worn down, so it didn't much matter that this second match was starting immediately following the first.

The first move was made by Solomon as he tried to close his arms around Swenson; but the younger man scooted away, and Solomon grabbed air.

The crowd was making so much noise that none of what they were shouting was understandable. It simply sounded like a loud roar, like thunder.

Solomon closed in on Swenson again, but the younger man was staying out of his reach.

Suddenly, Swenson darted forward, then fell to the ground. Most of the onlookers thought he had tripped over his own feet, but the fall was by design. While he was on the ground, he used both of his feet to hook one of Solomon's ankles and pull it out from under him. Solomon was suddenly on the ground, something no one else had been able to do.

Swenson moved quickly, leaping on Solomon with all his weight, trying to pin him. He managed to roll the big man over onto his stomach and then sat on the small of his back, hooking his chin as he had done with Murphy.

There, however, the similarity ended.

As Swenson pulled back on Solomon's chin, hoping to

force him to give up, Solomon pulled his knees up under him and laid his palms flat on the ground. He managed to work his way to his hands and knees, with Swenson still riding his back.

"Swenson's got Solomon now," Pike said.

"No," McConnell said, "Solomon's getting to his feet. If he does, Swenson will lose his advantage, and you'll lose your money."

Solomon's powerful thighs went to work as the big man worked hard at straightening up, even with Swenson on his back, holding on for dear life.

As Solomon straightened up, Swenson was about to let go and jump free when the big man drove himself backward, taking Swenson to the ground beneath him. Swenson hit the hard-packed dirt with Solomon on top of him, and everyone heard the air whoosh out of his lungs.

Solomon rolled free of Swenson, then turned over and dropped himself on top of the younger man again, pinning him.

"That's a pin!" Whiskey Sam cried out. "Solomon wins."

Twenty-Nine

When Swenson didn't move, Pike and some of the others rushed forward and, lifting him gingerly, carried him to a nearby tent where they could examine him.

"Here's the problem," Pike said. "When he fell backward, he hit his head on the ground."

At that point Caroline and Gloria both entered the tent. Caroline was carrying a pan of water, and Gloria an armful of cloths.

"Move, Pike," Caroline said.

Pike stood up and let the two women clean the bleeding lump on the back of Swenson's head. As he stepped outside, Solomon confronted him.

"Is he all right?" he asked.

"I think he'll be all right, Solomon."

"I didn't mean to hurt him," the big man said.

"Everybody knows that, Solomon," Pike said, putting his hand on the man's shoulders. "Why don't you go and get cleaned up?"

"Yeah, okay," Solomon said, and glumly walked away.

"He's really upset," McConnell observed, coming up next to Pike. He was accompanied by Whiskey Sam, who had apparently shaved a second time. Pike was impressed with the way the older man was handling the badge of authority that had been thrust on him.

"Yeah, I guess he doesn't know his strength."

"How's the kid?" Whiskey Sam asked.

"Caroline and Gloria are cleaning his head. If they can stop the bleeding, he should be all right, but he won't be wrestling for a while. I wouldn't be surprised if he's got some broken ribs as well."

"What happened to all those fancy moves?" McConnell asked.

"He was doing okay for a few minutes, but once Solomon fell on him, it was all over. I owe you five dollars."

McConnell waved it away. "Whenever."

At that point Gloria came out of the tent, followed by Caroline. Pike and McConnell couldn't help but compare the two women. They both had fair skin and large, firm breasts, but there the similarity ended. Gloria was short with a tendency toward chubbiness, while Caroline was taller and more slender. As far as age went, they were comparable, both somewhere in their late twenties.

And they were both lovely.

Pike couldn't help but think, if only Caroline wasn't married. . . .

McConnell couldn't help thinking, if only Gloria wasn't a whore. . . .

"How is he?"

"He's coming around," Gloria said, "but I don't think he should be on his feet for a while."

"Who's tent is this?" Caroline asked.

Pike and McConnell exchanged glances. They didn't know.

"Well, he's going to have to stay someplace," Gloria said. "Does he have a tent of his own?"

Pike looked at McConnell, and knew the answer to that one.

"No. The tents were first come."

"He's got to stay someplace," Gloria repeated.

Pike and McConnell exchanged another glance, and McConnell nodded.

"All right," Pike said, "we'll get a few men to carry him over to our tent. He'll stay there until he can get back on his feet."

For a moment Caroline's face revealed her displeasure with that setup, and then she said, "Let me make sure he's stopped bleeding," and went back inside.

"Not happy," McConnell said to Pike.

"Tough," Pike said.

"Did I miss something?" Gloria asked.

"Never mind," Pike said. "It's not important—but the question is a good one, Gloria."

"Huh? Oh, you mean . . . did I see the man who fought with Fitzsimmons?"

Pike nodded.

"I'm sorry, I must have seen at least eight dog soldiers, but I really couldn't tell."

"All right," Pike said, "I'll just have to question them individually."

"I'm really sorry."

"Don't be," Pike said. "You were very helpful today."

"Come on," McConnell said, "I'll walk you back to your tent."

"I hope you find the real killer, Pike," Gloria said. "I know you didn't do it."

Pike smiled at her. "Thanks, Gloria, that means a lot."

As McConnell and Gloria left, Pike and Whiskey Sam

grabbed three men and had them carry Swenson to Pike's tent.

Caroline watched as Swenson was carried away, and as Pike started to follow, she took hold of his arm with surprising strength.

"Where are we going to meet now?" she demanded.

"Caroline . . . I don't know if it's a good idea for us to . . . to meet again."

"That's funny," she said, "I think it's a wonderful idea. I had a fight with my husband today."

"Not over me, I hope."

"You were mentioned."

"Caroline, I'm sorry . . ." Pike said. "Look, we'll have to talk later."

"Yes," Caroline said, releasing his arm, "we will."

"Is Pike involved with Caroline?" Gloria asked as they reached her tent.

"I think it's the other way around," McConnell said.

"It's got to be both ways, Skins," Gloria said. "If they've had sex, I'm sure she didn't force him."

"No," McConnell said, "you're right about that."

"Your friend's going to get hurt if he's in love with her."

"Why do you say that?"

"She doesn't love him."

"How can you tell?"

She smiled. "I can tell. She wants him, but she doesn't love him."

"Well, I don't think he loves her, Gloria—or couldn't you tell that?"

"I never got a good look at him when he was looking

at her, but I'll take your word for it. Still, her being married and all, I would think that he wouldn't need the extra complications—not when he's suspected of killing Fitzsimmons."

"I think he's beginning to think the same thing," McConnell said.

When Swenson's eyes fluttered open, he looked up at Pike.

"You cost me five dollars," Pike said to him.

Swenson blinked, then frowned as he tried to remember what had happened.

"I'll try and make it up to you," he said.

"How do you feel?"

"Like I been beat against a rock and wrung out," Swenson said. "What happened?"

He started to get up, but Pike put his hand on his chest to stop him. "Solomon fell on you."

Swenson frowned. "I remember. Jesus, my head—"

"Yeah, you hit it when you fell," Pike said. "What else hurts?"

"I don't—" Swenson began, trying to move. "Ohh . . . my ribs."

"They might be cracked," Pike said. "You'll have to stay off your feet for a while."

"Where am I?"

"My tent, in my cot," Pike said. "You can stay here until you feel up to getting up."

"My skins," Swenson said. "I've got to sell my skins. . . ."

"I can do that for you," Pike said. "Who were you leaning toward dealing with?"

"The fella from Hudson's Bay."

"Mike Boone."

"Yeah, that's him."

"Boone's a good man. He'll give you a fair price."

"That's good to hear. How's Solomon?"

"He's all right. A little upset that you got hurt."

"That's nice of him."

"What happened to all that fancy leverage you were going to use?"

"It's kind of hard to use leverage when a man that size is falling on you."

"I guess."

"He's very strong," Swenson said, "but I still think I can beat him."

"Yeah, well," Pike said, "how about waiting till next rendezvous to try again?"

Swenson groaned as he shifted his head and said, "Good idea."

Thirty

Pike left Swenson to rest in his tent and went out looking for Bridger. He found him in the saloon tent, having a beer.

"Heard the way the wrestling match turned out," Bridger said. "How's the kid?"

"He'll live."

"It's too bad. I really thought he'd take Solomon."

"Did you bet on him?"

"Well," Bridger said, "I wasn't that sure. Come on, I'll buy you a beer."

Pike moved up to the bar and accepted the beer from the bartender.

"I found out some things you ought to know," Pike said.

"Like what?"

Pike told Bridger what McConnell had told him about the fight Gloria had seen.

"So you figure one of the dog soldiers killed him."

"I'm not figuring anything," Pike said. "All I know is Fitzsimmons had a fight with a dog soldier. I want to find that man and question him."

"Well," Bridger said, "what are we waiting for?" He

drained his beer and put the empty mug down on the bar. "There can't be more than a dozen of them."

Pike sipped his beer and put it back on the bar more full than empty. He caught up to Bridger outside, and they split the camp in half.

Pike gave Bridger the half with Caroline Hennessy in it.

The dog soldier spoke with Jack Pike, the man who had whipped Fitzsimmons in a fair fight. The dog soldier wished he could have done so as well.

Pike was asking all of the dog soldiers if they knew Fitzsimmons, and what kind of problems they had had with him. All of them said the same things, that they didn't like Fitzsimmons, but that they had to respect the fact that he was booshway.

The dog soldier had heard about the questions from other camp guards before Pike got to him, so he had his answers all ready. On the other side of the camp, Pike's friend Bridger was asking the same question and getting the same answers.

The dog soldier was sorry that he had to lie to Pike, but there was no other way.

Pike and Bridger met up that evening to exchange information.

"Nothing," Bridger said.

"That's what I got," Pike said glumly. "They're all so stolid that I couldn't even tell if one of them was lying."

"I know. It was like talking to one stone wall after another."

"Come on," Pike said. "My throat's dry from asking so many questions."

"The same questions," Bridger said, "and getting the same answers."

When they each had a beer and were sitting at a barrel, Bridger said, "We spoke to them all. What else can we do but ask them?"

"We could threaten them."

"Could we?"

"No, I guess not," Pike said. "We'd be threatening too many innocent men to get to the guilty one."

"So what's next?" Bridger asked.

"We can't give up," Pike said. "Gloria says she definitely saw an altercation between Fitzsimmons and a dog soldier,"

"What did she actually see?"

"A fight, although she said it was pretty much one sided in Fitzsimmons' favor."

"And she can't point out the dog soldier?"

Pike shook his head. "We gave her a good look at them today. She says the fight took place at night. All she knows for sure is that it *was* Fitzsimmons and a dog soldier she saw fighting."

"So what's our next move?"

Pike drummed his fingers for a few moments, then said, "I think we need twelve men who'd be willing to help us—or rather, me."

"Do you think there are that many men who believe you're innocent?"

"I think we're about to find out."

* * *

Pike secured permission from the owner of the saloon tent to hold a meeting there after closing, and then he and Bridger set about finding out if there were indeed twelve men at rendezvous who believed him and would be willing to help him.

There were.

After the saloon closed, Pike and Bridger met there with Whiskey Sam, Rocky Victor, Jim Cooper, Skins McConnell, Bob Mack, Will Murphy, and Solomon Fine. Also in attendance were mountain men Eddy Gorman, Wayne Dundee, Frankie Roderus and Johnny Lutz. A surprise attendee was Mike Boone, the Hudson's Bay Fur Company representative.

"Mike," Pike said as Boone arrived, "what are you doing here?"

"I heard there was a meeting here tonight to try to help you out, Pike," Boone said. "It's not only open to mountain men, is it?"

"No, no, of course not," Pike said, smiling. "Glad to have you, Mike."

When everyone was there, McConnell placed himself at the entrance, and Bridger and Pike stood up.

Pike explained his plan, that he needed twelve men, one each to follow the dog soldiers around.

"What do you expect that to accomplish?" Whiskey Sam asked.

Pike told them about finding out that Fitzsimmons had had a fight with a dog soldier shortly before he died.

"Have you talked to the dog soldiers?" Whiskey Sam asked.

Pike had the feeling that Whiskey Sam had actually attended the meeting in his capacity as booshway, as well as in his capacity as a friend.

"We have," Bridger said. "None of them admits to having a fight with him."

"So now you want to have them followed."

"That's right, Sam," Pike said. "I think the guilty man might get nervous and make a mistake, maybe give himself away."

Whiskey Sam thought about it and then said, "Sounds like as good an idea as any."

"Then we have your okay, as booshway?"

"Sure," Sam said, "and just tell me which one of them you want me to follow."

"No, not you, Sam," Pike said.

"Why not?"

"You've got other things to do."

Sam looked around and then said, "Without me, and not counting yourself and Bridger, you've only got eleven men."

Pike looked around the room himself, taking count, and found that Sam was right.

"I'll just have to get another man," Pike said, "or else Bridger or I will do it."

"There won't be any need for that," a voice called out.

Everyone turned to see who had spoken, and standing just inside the tent entrance was Hal Swenson.

"I'm your number twelve."

"You shouldn't even be on your feet, Swenson," Pike admonished.

As if to illustrate that point, Swenson wobbled suddenly. Skins McConnell reached for him, but Solomon Fine was even faster, probably driven by guilt. He was at the younger man's side, propping him up.

"Solomon, take him back to my tent," Pike said.

Solomon nodded.

"I'll be all right in the morning, Pike," Swenson said. "I'm your number twelve. Don't forget."

"I won't forget, Swenson."

Solomon helped Swenson out of the tent, and everyone turned around to look at Pike again.

"All right," Pike said. "I've got my twelve. Is there anyone here who isn't willing to go along with this hair-brained scheme?"

No one withdrew his support.

"Then you might as well all get a good night's sleep. Thanks for coming. In the morning we'll show you which dog soldier to follow."

Everyone filed out with the exception of Pike, Bridger, McConnell and Whiskey Sam.

Whiskey Sam approached Pike and said, "Let me help, Pike."

"You helped by being here, Sam, but you're booshway. You've got to be impartial."

"Oh, the hell with that—"

"Look," Pike said, cutting him off, "a lot of people laughed when you became booshway. They didn't think you could do the job, and to tell you the honest truth, I'm not sure I did, either."

"I know that—"

"But you've done a hell of a job, Sam," Pike continued, "a hell of a job, and you're going to continue to do so."

Whiskey Sam eyed Pike for a few moments and then said, "You know, this job ain't all it's cracked up to be. Did you know that I ain't been drunk since I became booshway?"

"I know, Sam," Pike said, "I know, and that's what I mean. You haven't been drunk, and you've been a damned good booshway."

"Thanks, Pike," Sam said. "Thanks."

Whiskey Sam left, and Pike turned to Bridger and McConnell.

"Do we have enough time to pull this off?" McConnell asked. "There are only two full days left in rendezvous. Is that enough time to break down a dog soldier?"

"Maybe not an innocent dog soldier," Pike said, "but I think it's more than enough time to work on a guilty one."

At least, he hoped so.

Thirty-One

The next morning Pike and Bridger split the twelve men, each taking six and splitting the camp in two halves. As a dog soldier passed them, Bridger and Pike would nod, and one of the men would break away and begin to follow.

Eventually, Pike had only Swenson left with him.

"Look, Hal, are you sure you're up to this?" Pike asked him.

"Sure," Swenson said. "I've got a little headache, but other than that I'm fine. I really appreciate you letting me use your tent and cot."

"I hope you're not just doing this to try and pay me back for that."

"Hell, no," Swenson said. "I don't happen to think you killed Fitzsimmons, Pike. I'd like to try and help you prove who did."

"I appreciate that. Okay, here comes your dog soldier. Stay with him."

"Like I was his shadow.

The dog soldier noticed the man following him right away. He was the young man who had tried to wrestle

Solomon. The dog soldier did not remember ever having exchanged words with the young man, so he could not understand why he would be following him.

The dog soldier decided to ignore the man, in the hope that maybe he would just go away.

Caroline Hennessy had gone to Pike's tent that night during the meeting. She had entered the tent and found it empty. As she left, she saw two men coming toward the tent and hid from view. She watched as Solomon helped Swenson into the tent, and then she went back to hers.

The next morning she went looking for Pike and found him just after he had parted company with Swenson.

"I went to your tent last night," she said. "You weren't there." Her tone was accusing.

"I had a meeting to attend."

"With who?" she asked. "That chubby blonde from the saloon?"

Pike frowned. He didn't need to have this kind of problem. If he hadn't been so angry the other night, he would have realized that and sent Caroline back to her own tent. He was sorry now that he hadn't.

"Caroline . . . even if I was with Gloria, that wouldn't be any of your business, but I wasn't."

"So you say."

"Caroline, I'm sure your husband needs you at the—"

"My husband doesn't need me, Pike," she said, "and I don't need him. What I need is you."

"Caroline, I don't love—"

She laughed then, surprising him. "I'm not talking about love, Pike," she said. "I'm talking about need."

"Well, then, I don't need you."

"That's not the point, either," she said. "*I* need *you.* I need what you gave me the other night."

"Caroline . . . we can't do again what we did the other night."

"But Pike, I—"

Lowering his voice, he said, "This is not the place to talk about this."

"Then meet me later."

"I can't."

"You mean you won't."

"Caroline—"

"I think I see," she said then. "You got what you wanted from me the other night, and now you want to move on to someone else, like your blonde friend."

"She's not *my* friend . . . Caroline, this has to stop."

"Oh, it's going to stop, all right, Pike," she said, "and you're going to be sorry. You're going to be so damned sorry!"

To his relief, she turned on her heel and walked away very quickly, her back held very stiffly. He looked around to see if their exchange had been witnessed by anyone. There were a few people in the area, but no one seemed to be paying him any special attention.

He hoped that he was finished with Caroline Hennessy.

Caroline Hennessy went back to her tent and walked in while her husband was conducting business.

"Caroline, I think I could use some help—"

"Later, Arthur," she said, and walked past him into the rear of the tent.

In the back she sat on her cot, her hands closed into fists and held at her sides.

Who did Jack Pike think he was, using her—and using her *once*—and then throwing her away in favor of some fat, blonde whore?

Well, if he thought he could do that to her and get away with it, he was sadly mistaken. He was going to pay for treating her like some one-night whore.

All she had to do was come up with a way to make him pay, and pay dearly.

And she thought she knew how. . . .

Thirty-Two

Whiskey Sam's squaw grunted or groaned each time he drove himself into her. This was the second time this morning that he was taking her. He thought back to his comment to Pike last night that the job of booshway was not all it was cracked up to be, but it did have its benefits. Ever since he had taken on the post as booshway and decided to do a proper job of it—cleaning himself up, remaining sober—he had, for some reason, regained some of the vigor of his youth.

"Ohhh!" the squaw cried out in pleasure, bringing her meaty thighs up and closing them around his almost frail form.

He drove into her again, and suddenly she was bucking beneath him, her large breasts flopping about on her chest, her chunky butt striking the hard floor beneath the blanket.

Whiskey Sam became mindless in his quest for his own release and slammed into her ruthlessly until finally he cried out as his release came. . . .

* * *

Pike and Bridger virtually took up residence in the saloon tent, waiting for some word from one of their men.

"It's not going to happen today," Pike said.

"Maybe not," Bridger said, "but what else would you suggest we do today?"

Pike shook his head. "If this doesn't work, I'm at a loss about what to do next."

"And so," Bridger said, "we wait. Would you like another beer?"

"May I speak to you?"

Whiskey Sam looked in embarrassment at the woman who had just entered the tent. Had she entered a moment earlier, she would have found him astride his squaw. Luckily, they had both managed to dress before she entered.

"I'm Caroline Hennessy," the woman said.

"I know who you are, ma'am," Sam said. He looked at his squaw who was still flushed from their exertions. "Let's go outside."

Caroline nodded, and preceded Whiskey Sam out of the tent.

"What can I do for you, Mrs. Hennessy?"

"I . . . I'm afraid I have some information that I've . . . I've been holding back from you."

"Holdin' back? Why?"

"I . . . I'd rather not say, right now."

"What information are you talking about?"

"Well, it has to do with . . . with the death of Mr. Fitzsimmons."

Whiskey Sam stopped walking. "What are you talkin' about?" he asked.

"I saw a man go into Mr. Fitzsimmons tent last night," she said, facing Whiskey Sam. "A man carrying a knife."

"You did?"

"Yes."

This was what Pike needed, Sam thought excitedly. A witness to prove his innocence once and for all.

"Did you recognize him?"

"I did."

"Well damn it, woman—" he began, then stopped himself and asked her calmly, "why didn't you come forward with information before?"

"I didn't want to . . . to make trouble for him."

"Make trouble . . . Mrs. Hennessy, who did you see that night?"

She hesitated a moment and then said, "It was Jack Pike."

"What?"

"I saw Jack Pike go into Fitzsimmons' tent with a knife in his hand," Caroline Hennessy said. "Pike killed him."

"She said what?"

They were in the saloon, Pike, Bridger, and Whiskey Sam, and Sam had just told Pike what Caroline Hennessy had said.

"She said you killed him," Sam repeated.

"Did she say she saw me do it?"

"No," Whiskey Sam said. 'She said she saw you go into his tent with a knife."

"She's lying."

"Why?"

Pike looked at Bridger, and then to Sam. He told them why she would lie.

"So she's saying this just to get back at you?"

"I think so."

Whiskey Sam shook his head. "I'm not a lawman, Pike. To tell you the truth, I don't know what to do with this information."

"I don't think she wants to do anything with it, Sam," Pike said.

"So what's her game?' Bridger asked.

"She wants the word to get around, that's all. She wants to make me *look* as guilty as hell."

"Just to get back at you, she wants to brand you a killer?" Bridger asked. "This must be one helluva mean woman, Pike. What did you see in her?"

"The obvious, Bridger," Pike said, "just the obvious."

"Pike, rendezvous is over tomorrow night," Sam said. "There's no way a lawman is gonna get back here in time. I knew that when I sent a man for him. You can just ride out. No lawman is gonna go looking for you, and even if he did, he'd never find you in the mountains if you didn't want to be found."

"It's not the law I'm worried about, Sam," Pike said. "It's the rest of these people here at rendezvous. It's the people who will be here next year and the year after that—if rendezvous goes on that long. I can't leave here with people thinking I might be a murderer."

"So what do I do?" Sam asked.

"There's no proof that Pike killed Fitzsimmons," Bridger said. "You've done what you had to do; you faced Pike with the accusation."

"Now what?" Sam asked.

"Now we wait and see what happens with Pike's plan," Bridger said.

"If one of those dog soldiers is guilty," Pike said. "He'll

crack, and then it won't matter what Caroline Hennessy says."

"I hope you're right," Whiskey Sam said.

Yeah, Pike thought, so do I.

The dog soldier decided that the man following him must have suspected him of killing Fitzsimmons. For that reason, the dog soldier decided that he had to kill another white man.

He'd wait until the middle of the night, when the man would be asleep, and then he would have to kill him the same way he killed Fitzsimmons.

And for the same reason.

To protect his reputation.

Swenson was feeling lousy.

He knew that he should probably have remained on his back for a couple more days, but there was only that much time left in rendezvous—his first rendezvous—and he didn't want to waste it on his back.

Besides, Pike needed help, and Swenson wanted to be one of the men who helped him. Swenson had heard a lot about Pike, and it had been Pike who had come to his aid when he'd needed it, after his accidental injury.

Swenson was cold because he was sweating and the cold mountain air felt even colder on his wet brow. He wondered if he had a fever and hoped that he wouldn't end up fainting.

He followed his dog soldier and watched his every move until it was well after midnight. A couple of dog soldiers remained on patrol during the night; but his had already turned in, so he decided that it was time for him to do the same.

What could happen during the night?

Thirty-Three

"I wouldn't go and see her," Skins McConnell warned Pike.

"Why not?" Pike asked.

They were in their tent, which they had back to themselves. Despite their offer, Swenson had decided to go back to sleeping under the stars.

"That's what she wants," McConnell said. "She wants you chasing her down, for whatever reason. Just stay away from her, Pike. You don't need the extra complication in your life. When she sees you're ignoring her, she'll change her story."

"I don't agree," Pike said. "I think if I ignore her she'll get even angrier."

"That may be, but if it looks like you're after her because of what she said, it may give some people the idea that she's right."

"Then I'm damned if I do and damned if I don't."

"Face it," McConnell said. "The only way out of this is to find out who killed Fitz."

"Well shit, that's what we've been trying to do, but if this plan doesn't work, I don't know what to do next."

"Well, let's hope that it works, then. Let's get some sleep and see what tomorrow brings."

"I guess you're right. . . ."

Pike couldn't sleep, however, and eventually he got up and went out to take a walk. Maybe the cold, middle of the night, Rocky Mountain air would clear his mind so he could come up with another idea.

The dog soldier found where the white man who was following him was sleeping. He had his knife ready, but the man was not sleeping in an isolated area. Instead, many men had staked out a place at the north end of the camp and pitched their bedrolls. There was no way the dog soldier could get near the white man with all of the other men around him.

He was going to have to wait for an opportunity during the day tomorrow to get rid of his threat.

The dog soldier turned away, knife in hand, and came face-to-face with Jack Pike.

"Dog soldier," Pike said, "we have to have a talk."

"I have nothing to talk about," the dog soldier said.

"What are you doing out here?"

"I am on patrol."

Pike shook his head.

"I saw two dog soldiers on patrol already, my friend. Try another story."

"I do not know what you mean by a story," the dog soldier said. His knife was still in his hand, and Pike kept a wary eye on it.

"Why are you sneaking around out here with a knife in your hand?"

The dog soldier looked down accusingly at the knife he still held, as if it were somehow giving him away.

"What's going on?"

Pike looked past the dog soldier and saw Hal Swenson standing there. Swenson's face was sticky with sweat, and his eyes were glazed. It was plain to Pike that the man had a high temperature.

"This the dog soldier you've been following?"

"It is."

"He's been sneaking around out here with this pig sticker in his hand. I think maybe we got the reaction we were looking for, Swenson. What do you think?"

"I think—" Swenson said, and suddenly his eyes rolled up into his head, and he keeled over.

At that exact moment, the dog soldier lunged for Pike with the knife. Having been cut once that week, and finding once enough, Pike moved quickly. He sidestepped the lunge, and as the dog soldier's arm went by, Pike dropped his elbow on it, breaking the forearm. The dog soldier screamed, dropped his knife, and went to his knees, cradling his injured arm.

Pike went to Swenson's aid, and as the dog soldier's scream woke the other men who were sleeping in the area, he called for some help in getting Swenson and the dog soldier to the saloon tent. He also asked someone to go and get Whiskey Sam and Jim Bridger.

Maybe, he thought, he was finally going to get some answers and finally throw off the mantle of suspicion he had been wearing ever since Fitzsimmons' death.

Thirty-Four

The saloon tent looked as if it were open for business, there were so many people milling about.

"Maybe I should start serving drinks," the owner said to McConnell.

"Naw, we're gonna clear it out," McConnell said. "Besides, that'd be kind of hard with Swenson stretched out on your bar."

Both the owner and McConnell looked over to where Gloria was tending to Swenson, bathing his forehead with cold cloths in an attempt to bring his fever down.

On the floor, cradling his shattered forearm, was the dog soldier whose head was now covered with as much perspiration as Swenson's was.

"Let's get this place cleared out a little," Bridger suggested to Whiskey Sam. "Most of these people are just curious."

"Right," Whiskey Sam said. "Would you help me?"

"Sure."

Sam and Bridger went off to try and clear the tent.

Pike went to the bar to see how Swenson was doing.

"How is he?" he asked Gloria.

"He's burning up, but he's not quite as hot as he was

when you brought him in," she said. Then she glared at Pike. "He should never have been on his feet, not after that head injury."

"Don't blame me; I told him the same thing."

"If I could get him to my tent, I could bathe his entire body and not just his head. It would help get his fever down."

"I'll get you some men."

Pike went to the tent entrance, where men were now filing out, and grabbed two of them to carry Swenson to Gloria's tent.

Before Gloria could leave, Pike asked her to look at the injured man and see if she could identify him.

"I'm sorry," she said after studying the man for a few moments, "I can't say."

"All right," Pike said, "thanks."

Several minutes later, the tent was all but deserted. Even the owner had left, so that the only people in it now were Pike, Bridger, Whiskey Sam, McConnell and the injured dog soldier.

"What do you think?" Bridger asked Pike.

They were looking at the dog soldier, who was rocking back and forth, cradling his arm and moaning in pain. Pike had the man's knife tucked into his belt.

"I think he's in pain," Pike said, "but not as bad as he's making it seem."

"I agree," Bridger said. "I think we can get him to talk."

"How?" Whiskey Sam asked.

"Watch," Pike said.

Pike and Bridger approached the injured man while McConnell and Whiskey Sam hung back to watch.

"What's your name?" Pike asked.

The man didn't answer; he just rocked harder and crooned louder to his injured arm.

Pike bent over and said into the man's ear, "What is your name?"

Again the man didn't answer.

Pike took the man's knife out of his belt, reversed it so he was holding it by the blade, and then used the handle to tap the man soundly on the injured arm.

The man screamed, and Whiskey Sam groaned aloud and clutched his own arm, as if he could also feel the pain.

Pike waited until the man's moans became lower and then asked again, "What's your name?"

"Joe," the man gasped.

"Joe what?"

"Wingfoot."

"Joe Wingfoot," Pike said. "You're Crow, aren't you?"

"Yes."

As if Pike hadn't had enough trouble with the Crow this week.

"Did you kill the former booshway, Fitzsimmons?"

The man didn't answer.

Pike reached for his arm with the handle of the knife, and the man pulled it away so quickly that he bumped it himself on a nearby barrel and screamed again.

Again Pike waited until the waves of pain passed and had been reduced to a dull throb, then proceeded with his questions.

"You had a fight with Fitzsimmons, isn't that right?"

"No."

"We have a witness who saw you."

The man simply shook his head.

"Look, my friend, I can keep this up all night. Can you?" Pike asked.

The man looked up at Pike, and the pain he was feeling was evident in his eyes.

"Very well," he said softly. "I was in a fight with Fitzsimmons."

"He beat you, didn't he?"

"Yes."

"Badly?"

"He kicked me and spit on me."

Suddenly, it made sense to Pike. "Like a dog," he said to Wingfoot.

"Yes," Wingfoot said with feeling, "like a dog."

"So you killed him."

Wingfoot hesitated.

"You killed him, didn't you?"

Wingfoot hesitated again, then nodded. "Yes," he said softly—too softly for Whiskey Sam and McConnell to have heard him.

"Louder."

"Yes!" Wingfoot said. "I killed him!"

Pike turned around to look at Whiskey Sam, who nodded that he had heard. McConnell smiled at his friend, relieved.

Pike turned back to Wingfoot and asked, "How did you kill him?"

"I had to kill him," Wingfoot said, either misunderstanding the question, or saying what he felt he had to say. "I could not have fought him fairly and won, and yet I had to save face."

"By stabbing him in the back?" Bridger asked.

"I could not allow him to kick me and spit on me without paying," Wingfoot said. He looked at Bridger and Pike and asked, "Do you understand?"

"Sure," Bridger said. "Sure we can."

"How did you kill him?" Pike asked.

"I slipped into his tent and stabbed him."

"That's it, then," Bridger said. "Congratulations, Pike.

"Thanks," Pike said.

"I stabbed him," Wingfoot said again, "once in the back, but he was dead . . . oh yes, he was dead. I had to wait for the woman to leave. . . ."

The man kept talking, but Pike and Bridger and the others had heard what they needed to hear. Pike and Bridger walked over to where Whiskey Sam and McConnell were standing.

"Fitzsimmons always was a bully," McConnell said. "I guess he bullied the wrong man."

"A coward," Bridger said. "He stabbed a man in the back because he knew he couldn't beat him face-to-face, and he did it to save face."

"He was probably going to try and kill Swenson for the same reason."

"And the same way," Bridger said. "In the back, one swift, cowardly stroke."

"What are we going to do with him?" Whiskey Sam asked.

"Hold him," Pike said.

"For who?" McConnell asked. "By the time a lawman gets here, rendezvous will be long over. Who's going to wait here with him?"

"Maybe we should just tie him to a tree and let him wait on his own," Whiskey Sam said.

"He'd freeze to death," Pike said. "No man deserves that."

"No man deserves to be stabbed in the back, either," Bridger said. He was obviously in favor of leaving Wingfoot tied to a tree.

While the four of them tried to decide his fate, Joe Wingfoot decided to take matters into his own hands. Since it was now impossible for him to save face at all, he pulled himself to his feet and staggered around behind the bar.

"Hey!" Whiskey Sam said, spotting him. "What's he doing?"

While they all watched, Wingfoot took a whiskey bottle from behind the bar and shattered it against the bar.

"Look out—" Bridger said, pulling his pistol from his belt.

"Wait—" Pike said, putting his hand on Bridger's arm, and then he called out to Wingfoot, "No!"

Ignoring Pike, the Indian reversed the bottle and drove the jagged edge of it into his throat as hard as he could.

"Jesus!" McConnell said.

They rushed to the man's aid but the damage was much too extensive, and in moments the man had bled to death.

Thirty-Five

While Whiskey Sam and Bridger made arrangements to dispose of Joe Wingfoot's body, Pike and McConnell went to Gloria's tent.

Swenson was lying on Gloria's cot, and he was totally naked. She was bathing his body with cold cloths, and Swenson—despite his weakened conditon—was showing a fairly impressive erection.

"Looks to me like he's gonna be all right," McConnell said.

Gloria turned, and when she saw them, she tossed a blanket over Swenson's lower extremities.

"What happened?" Gloria asked.

"The dog soldier admitted killing Fitzsimmons," McConnell said.

"That's good."

"And then he killed himself," Pike said.

"Oh," she said, unsure how to react to that.

"Congratulations, Pike," Swenson said, turning his head to look at Pike.

"Thanks, Swenson," Pike said. "How are you feeling?"

"Better," he said, "thanks to Gloria."

"If you'd like, we can move back to our tent, where you can get some rest."

"I'd like to keep him here," Gloria said. She put her hand on Swenson's bare chest in a protective gesture. "He's going to need bathing through the night."

Pike shrugged and said, "Sure." Then he looked at McConnell, who also shrugged.

"Stay off your feet until this young lady says different," Pike said.

"Don't worry," Gloria said to him, "there will be other rendezvous."

Her hand was still on Swenson's hairless chest, and she was rubbing him gently. Pike thought that there was more than a simple wish on Gloria's part to nurse the man back to health. He looked at McConnell to see if his friend was seeing the same thing he was.

He was.

"Well," Pike said, "get some rest." He wasn't sure if he was talking to Swenson or Gloria.

"We'll see you tomorrow, Swenson," McConnell said.

"I'm glad things turned out well for you, Pike," Gloria said.

"Thank you, Gloria."

She smiled at him, and then he and McConnell backed out of the tent.

"Did you see what I saw?" Pike asked.

"Well," McConnell said, "that's a woman for you."

"At least she threw you over for a younger, better looking man."

McConnell made a face at his friend and said, "You can't get thrown over by a whore. Come on, let's get some sleep."

* * *

After Pike and McConnell left, Swenson looked at Gloria, who still had her hand on his chest.

"I want to thank you for what you're doing for me."

"It's nothing," she said, sliding her hand down his chest to his stomach.

He looked at her hand and said, "What—"

"I don't want you to be disappointed about being on you back on my cot," she said. She removed the blanket from his lower body and regarded his erection with interest.

"You're very beautiful, did you know that?" she asked. She leaned over and kissed his thigh.

"I—I never—you're beautiful, not me," Swenson stammered.

"No . . ." she said. She ran her mouth up and down his thighs, peppering them with hot, wet kisses until his cock was huge and throbbing. She made a ring out of her thumb and forefinger and dripped it down over his rigid penis; like a perfect throw in horseshoes. Sliding her fingers up and down the smooth length of him, she added, "It's you who are beautiful."

"Gloria—"

"Just lay still," she said, rising to her knees. "I'm going to make sure you don't mind being here."

Slowly she ran her tongue up and down his length, the ring of her fingers having fallen down to the base of his cock. She laved him until his cock glistened with her saliva, and then she took him into her hot mouth, he decided that he wasn't going to be disappointed at all.

Epilogue

I

The next morning Pike rose late and saw that McConnell had already left the tent. They had talked briefly the night before when they returned to their tent. The gist of the conversation was that neither one of them had ended up doing very well with women at this rendezvous—but then that wasn't so different from past rendezvous, either.

"Besides," Pike had said, "we don't come here looking for women, anyway."

"We don't?" McConnell asked.

"Well, not any that we'd want to take with us when we leave."

"You've got that much right."

"And when you think about it," Pike said, "we didn't do too badly. I mean, Caroline was pretty damn good."

"Gloria was *very* good," McConnell said.

"And you have to admit, young Swenson needs some cheering up right about now."

"That's true," McConnell said. "More power to him, I say . . ."

"That's real generous of you."

Now Pike rose and dressed quickly. Thinking of Caroline Hennessy last night had reminded him that he still had something to clear up. Whatever her reasons were, he didn't like the idea that she had lied about him.

He was going to go over and talk to her, even if it meant he'd have to talk to her husband.

Arthur Hennessy wasn't happy.

As many threats as he had made in his mind against Pike, he realized that he had not had the courage to carry any of them out. He would never have the courage that kind of action needed, not against a man like Pike.

This was the last day of rendezvous. All he could hope was that Caroline would decide to return with him to St. Louis.

At least he'd had a good trip businesswise.

He was helping a man who needed some supplies when Jack Pike walked in. Hennessy looked at Pike once, then looked away as he continued to help his customer.

Pike approached the counter, and Hennessy just looked at him and said, "She's in the back."

Pike looked surprised and then nodded and stepped to the back.

He entered the Hennessy's sleeping area and found Caroline packing.

"Caroline," he said, and she turned, astonished to see him.

"Well," she said, "if you've decided that you want me, you're too late."

"I don't want you," he said bluntly. "I want to know why you lied about me?"

"Did I?"

"You should know that we found the man who killed Dan Fitzsimmons," he said. "So your lie has been wasted."

She dropped the article of clothing she had been about to pack and whirled on him angrily.

"You rejected me!"

"Hasn't that ever happened before?"

"No!"

"Well then I'm sorry I had to be the first, but I didn't want to get involved with you right from the beginning."

"You weren't fighting so hard a couple of nights ago," she pointed out.

"That was wrong, Caroline," he said. "I was angry about something, and you came along—it was just wrong."

"How could it have been wrong and felt so good?" she demanded.

"I'm sorry, Caroline," he said, "I don't know what to say to you."

Angrily she said, "Well, if you're waiting for an apology, forget it."

"No," he said, "I don't know why I came here. I really didn't expect an apology."

She was so angry now that it contorted her face to the point where she was no longer beautiful.

"I'm sorry . . ." he said, and left.

"Don't turn your back on me!" she shouted shrilly, and Pike turned just in time to see her coming at him with the knife.

She had it high over her head and looked like she had every intention of driving it into his back. He caught her wrist and bent it backward until she cried out in pain and dropped the knife.

Arthur Hennessy came running in just as Pike released her arm, and she slumped to the ground, holding her wrist.

"What's going on?"

"He hurt me, Arthur," she said to her husband. "Make him pay. Make him pay!"

Arthur Hennessy looked at Pike warily, and Pike spoke before the smaller man had time to build up the courage to make a mistake.

"You know she's sick, don't you?"

"I know it," Hennessy admitted. "What are you going to do?"

Pike knew what he *should* do, and that was turn her over to the nearest law, but she *was* sick, and that meant she needed help which she wouldn't get in a jail cell.

"I'm going to let you take her home, Hennessy," Pike said finally, hoping he was doing the right thing. "Take your wife home and get her some help."

"I will," Hennessy said. "I swear it."

Hennessy rushed to his wife's side as Pike turned and walked out.

Outside, Pike thought about the dog soldier who'd killed himself. Although the man had tried to kill Fitzsimmons, he had succeeded only in stabbing a man who was already dead. That meant he had died for nothing. Pike couldn't feel sorry for him, though. After all, he had *tried* to commit murder.

In the end, he couldn't feel sorry for the dog soldier or for Caroline Hennessy.

However, he did have plenty of sympathy for Arthur Hennessy . . . who probably needs it, and a lot more.

II

Pike spent the rest of the day saying goodbye to people—many of whom apologized for having suspected him of killing Fitzsimmons—and also closed his deal for his skins with Mike Boone of Hudson's Bay.

"Did you ever find a partner of Fitzsimmons?" Boone asked.

"No. Why?"

"I heard that he had a source for beaver pelt."

"He was making a deal with Fleming."

"Yeah, well, I would have made a deal for them as well," Boone said. "You can't hold that against Fleming. Fitzsimmons would have undercut the rest of you because he had an overabundance of pelts."

"I guess there are a lot of beaver who are safe today," Pike said.

Boone laughed and agreed.

Pike found Bridger and McConnell in the saloon.

"Anybody see Swenson this morning?" he asked, joining them when he had gotten himself a beer.

"Haven't seen Swenson or Gloria," McConnell said. "I don't think they've come out of her tent yet."

"That boy ain't gonna be able to walk right," Bridger

said, "and it's gonna have nothing to do with a head injury."

All three of them laughed, pleased that rendezvous was almost over. They could all begin to look forward to next year and hope it was better than this year."

"Where's Whiskey Sam?"

"Strutting around here somewhere," McConnell said, "enjoying his last day as booshway."

"You think he'll revert to form after this?" Bridger asked.

"That's an interesting question," McConnell said. "Being booshway sure did change him, didn't it?"

"Into a whole new man," Bridger said.

Bridger looked at Pike, intending to ask what he thought, but Pike was staring off into space, his thoughts obviously somewhere else. Bridger looked at McConnell, who simply shrugged his shoulders.

"Hey!" McConnell said.

"He didn't kill him," Pike said.

"What?" Bridger said.

"Damn it!" Pike said, pounding his hand down on the barrel top, spilling a generous portion of everybody's beer. "Wingfoot didn't kill Fitzsimmons."

"What are you talking about?" McConnell asked. "He said he stabbed him."

"Sure, he stabbed him, but he didn't kill him."

"I don't get it," Bridger said, exchanging helpless glances with McConnell.

"He killed a dead man," Pike said, as if that would clear the whole thing up.

"Oh," McConnell said, "well, at least now you're making sense." He stared at Pike as if he had sprouted a third eye.

"Fitzsimmons was already dead when Wingfoot stabbed him."

"Why do you say that?"

"How many times was Fitz stabbed?"

"Twice," Bridger said.

"How many times did Wingfoot say he stabbed him?"

Both Bridger and McConnell shrugged.

"Once," Pike said, "he said he stabbed him once. He also said he had to wait for the woman to leave."

"I didn't hear that," McConnell said, looking at Bridger, who shook his head.

"You fellas had stopped listening by then."

"Do you really know what you're talking about?" Bridger asked. "Do you have proof that Wingfoot didn't stab Fitzsimmons twice?"

Pike thought a moment, then brightened and said excitedly, "Yes, I do. Come on!"

He jumped up and ran from the tent, with Bridger and McConnell bringing up a puzzled rear.

III

They followed Pike to the shallow grave they had dug for Fitzsimmons and found him on his hands and knees, digging the dirt away.

"You don't want to do that," McConnell said.

"Yes," Pike said, "I do. I need the blanket.'

"What blanket?" Bridger asked.

"The blanket he slept with. The one we buried him with. Come on, help me!"

Again—for what seemed like the hundredth time in the past five minutes—Bridger and McConnell exchanged puzzled glances.

"We'd better humor him," McConnell said.

They got to their knees and helped Pike dig until they came to the body.

"Okay, I need the blanket," Pike said. He found the end of the blanket and then yanked on it mightily. The body spun around two or three times, and the blanket came loose in his hands. He stood up with his prize.

"Now what?" McConnell asked, standing up.

"Look," Pike said, holding the blanket out to them.

"At what?" Bridger asked.

"This," Pike said, and he poked his fingers through the slit that Wingfoot's knife had made in the blanket.

"Did you expect him to stab him through the blanket without making a hole?" Bridger asked.

"Do you think he stabbed Fitz twice through the blanket and made only one hole?"

Bridger opened his mouth to reply, then stopped as the import of what Pike said hit him.

"Maybe," McConnell said lamely, "he stabbed him twice through the same hole."

"And maybe," Pike said, "he stabbed him once, then put the blanket over him and stabbed him again. Or maybe he stabbed him through the blanket, then uncovered him and stabbed him again, and then covered him so he wouldn't get cold."

"All right, all right," Bridger said, "explain it."

"I will," Pike said. "Fitz had a woman in his tent with him."

"And she didn't see Wingfoot?" McConnell said.

"Shut up and listen!" Pike said. "She didn't see Wingfoot because she was already gone when Wingfoot got there. She had stabbed Fitzsimmons and left him for dead beneath the blankets. Wingfoot came in and stabbed a dead man!"

Bridger and McConnell didn't reply.

"That's why you've got one wound under the blanket," Pike said. "She stabbed him while they were having sex."

"A woman would have to be pretty sick—McConnell said, and then stopped.

All three men exchanged glances, and Pike thought about the knife Caroline McConnell had tried to use on him that afternoon.

"Oh my God," McConnell said. "Wingfoot died for nothing?"

"No, no," Pike said. "He did stab Fitz with intentions of killing him. It's not as if he didn't deserve what he got."

"And what about Mrs. Hennessy?" Bridger asked. "What does she deserve?"

"I don't know," Pike said. "Help me cover this poor bastard up."

While he covered Fitzsimmons again, Pike reasoned aloud that seeing Fitz take a beating from Pike must not have been enough for Caroline. She had to come to Fitz in the middle of the night, offer herself to him—she'd never been turned down, remember?—and then killed him either during sex, or after.

"Can we hold her?" Bridger asked.

"Can we prove this?" Pike asked. "And if we hold her, who do we hold her for? We're in the same predicament we were in with Wingfoot. Do we tie her to a tree?"

"Maybe she'll give us the same help Wingfoot did." McConnell suggested, only half kidding.

They finished burying Fitzsimmons and got to their feet, slapping dirt from their clothes, and then slapping their hands together.

"Or we let her go back to St. Louis," Pike said, "where she's bound to do something that the law will get her for."

"How do we know that?"

"Because she's sick," Pike said. "Sooner or later another man will try to force himself on her, or turn her down, and she'll go . . . crazy again."

"What if she decides to kill her husband?" Bridger asked.

Pike thought about that and said, "You're right. I'll have to warn that poor bastard so he doesn't end up like this poor bastard."

Pike started to walk away when Bridger called out, "What if he doesn't believe you?"

Pike turned, thought about it for a moment, and then shrugged. He didn't have an answer.

"Wait for me in the saloon," Pike said. "We might as well get rip roaring drunk our last night here."

"Is that gonna help?" Skins McConnell asked.

"I don't know," Jack Pike said, "but it can't hurt.